W9-AOQ-608

THE PUBLISHER GRATEFULLY ACKNOWLEDGES
THE GENEROUS CONTRIBUTION TO THIS BOOK
PROVIDED BY THE S. MARK TAPER
FOUNDATION.

"The First Day" and Other Stories

"The First Day"
and Other Stories

Dvora Baron

TRANSLATED BY

Naomi Seidman
with Chana Kronfeld

EDITED BY

Chana Kronfeld
and Naomi Seidman

UNIVERSITY OF CALIFORNIA PRESS

Berkeley   Los Angeles   London

University of California Press
Berkeley and Los Angeles, California

University of California Press, Ltd.
London, England

The story "Fradl" was previously published in Amia Leiblich,
Conversations with Dvora (Berkeley and Los Angeles: University
of California Press, 1997), and is reproduced here by permission.

Library of Congress Cataloging-in-Publication Data

Baron, Devorah, 1887–1956.
  [Short stories. English. Selections]
  "The first day" and other stories / Dvora Baron ; translated by
Naomi Seidman with Chana Kronfeld ; edited by Chana
Kronfeld and Naomi Seidman.
     p.   cm.
  ISBN 0-520-08536-1 (cloth : alk. paper)—ISBN 0-520-08538-8
(pbk. : alk. paper)
   1. Jews—Europe, Eastern—Social life and customs—Fiction.
I. Title.

PJ5053.B34 A27   2001
892.4'35—dc21   00-055162
                                   CIP

Manufactured in the United States of America
09 08 07 06 05 04 03 02 01
10 9 8 7 6 5 4 3 2 1

The paper used in this publication is both acid-free and totally
chlorine-free (TCF). The paper used in this publication meets the
minimum requirements of ANSI/NISO Z39.48-1992
(R 1997) (*Permanence of Paper*). ∞

To my mother, Sara Seidman

CONTENTS

TRANSLATOR'S
ACKNOWLEDGMENTS

Translation can never be entirely solitary work, but *The First Day* is a product of a particularly rich and intricate collaboration. Among the pleasures of working on this book was that it has brought me into close contact not only with Dvora Baron (my admiration for her has only intensified in the bright light of the translation workshop), but also with Chana Kronfeld. Chana is the teacher who first introduced me to Baron, the editor who recruited me to translate her, and the co-translator and friend with whom I spent a long summer in a series of Berkeley cafés (once even shouting over a blaring television set in a bar!), reading aloud and discussing nearly every word of the translation. Chana's sharp literary eye brought Baron alive for me, but she also made the work of translation more fun than that phrase might imply. Chana is the smartest, warmest, and most generous person I know; as happy as I am to finally send this manuscript off to press, I'm going to miss working with her.

There were many others who helped us along our way. Chana Bloch read our introduction and promptly faxed us four pages of astute comments. Our introduction and selection of stories heavily relied on the Israeli literary historian Nurit Govrin, who reintroduced Dvora Baron's early work and biography to the Hebrew-reading public. Amia Lieblich's psychobiography of Baron, translated as the companion volume to these stories, provided us with the impetus for this project. Doris Kretschmer ably guided the project through its difficult early stages at the University of California Press; Linda Norton brought it to completion. Eliyah Arnon worked on acquiring permissions and helped with the proofreading. Kathleen Van Sickle helped prepare the final manuscript. Eliezer Bryski helped with an early draft of "Ziva." Sheila Jelen, whose interest in Baron has paralleled my own, read and commented on drafts of some of the stories. David Biale, Dina Stein, and Rabbi Yoel Kahn helped me out with a few difficult phrases. John Schott and our son, Ezra, who was born midway through this project, were the source and goal of my energies.

Finally my mother, Sara Seidman, to whom this translation is dedicated, was beside me at every stage of this project. She worked on early drafts of five stories, was my constant consultant on Yiddish, on the intricacies of Eastern European culture, on aspects of Baron's religious world. This translation of Baron's stories became a precious meeting place for my mother and me, just as my mother's astonishing and powerful stories, impressed on my earliest consciousness, were the ground on which I encountered Baron. It is to my mother, native of Torda, Romania, and, like Baron, the daughter and granddaughter of rabbis and a master storyteller, that I dedicate this translation with deepest love.

Naomi Seidman

INTRODUCTION

When Dvora Baron, the first modern Hebrew woman writer, died in 1956 at the age of sixty-nine, she had not left her Tel Aviv apartment for thirty-three years. During the last twenty years, she was virtually confined to her bed, attended by her only daughter, Tsipora. She continued to write and translate, producing numerous stories as well as the definitive Hebrew translation of Flaubert's *Madame Bovary.* The circumstances of this self-imposed seclusion, and the part her daughter took in it, have never been fully established: there were health problems, for which she followed a strict dietary regimen of her own devising, resisting medical intervention; but Baron also implied that she was mourning the death of her brother, Benjamin, in the First World War. That Tsipora never attended school or made her own circle of friends, devoting herself completely to her mother, only deepens the mystery.

It is clear, though, that Baron's withdrawal from the society burgeoning all around her provided the space for a bold literary self-fashioning. In the winter of 1910–11 a combination of personal tragedy and Zionist passions had brought her to Palestine and the very center of the local Hebrew culture, as the literary editor of a Zionist-Socialist magazine. But the realities of pioneer life did not engage her for very long, least of all as a writer: she gradually turned inward, in her life and work. Baron spent the second half of her career as she had spent the first, writing and rewriting stories that were primarily drawn from the world of the Eastern European shtetl, the world of her childhood and adolescence. This was a preference little to the taste of her readers, who demanded literature that reflected the new society coming into being in Palestine. Like others of her generation, Baron had uprooted herself in the most dramatic way; her readers could not understand how she had then resisted, for the most part, moving her literary universe as well. Even the critics, who always acknowledged her gift for Hebrew prose, came to consider Baron somewhat old-fashioned, a "minor" writer who limited her repertoire to such insignificant themes as birth and death, marriage and divorce, rather than focusing on "important" matters, that is, the great national questions of the day. It was taken as a matter of course—against all evidence—that the eighty or so stories Baron published were more or less straightforward autobiographical "portraits." It didn't help that she wrote only one longer piece, a novella called "Exiles": short stories about the shtetl were not the stuff of literary nation building.

By contrast, when Baron first emerged on the Eastern European Hebrew literary scene in 1902, when she was just fourteen, her work created an immediate sensation, not only because of the author's youth but also because of her gender—until

Baron, Hebrew literature had been, as far as its readers knew, a strictly male province. Critics and fellow writers alike hailed the arrival of a major talent. Even readers who hadn't managed to get hold of the Hebrew journals in which Baron's first stories were published were fascinated by the rumors circulating about the existence of a Hebrew writer who was a rabbi's daughter: an early reader remembers her excitement at finding an issue with a story by Baron, describing how all her friends clamored to see it and devoured every word. One writer, eager to see the literary phenomenon with his own eyes, made a special trip to her shtetl. The story goes:

> As he came into town, Dvora Baron was standing barefoot at the well, vigorously washing the dishes. "Hey, little girl," the man approached her, "Can you tell me where the Baron family lives?" She pointed out the house. A few minutes later, her brother called to her excitedly: "Dvorka, it's you they came to see."

But the very precocity of Baron's work also aroused scandal: a few editors doubted that a nice Jewish girl could have written stories like these, suggesting that it must be a man hiding behind a female pen name (a common enough practice in Yiddish letters of the time); a few years later Baron's fiancé broke off their engagement, suspicious of the chastity of a young woman who could write so knowingly about love, and even sex. That a body of work can go from being too daring to being old-fashioned, without much changing its own course, tells us something about both the vagaries of literary taste and the paradoxical pulls within Baron's life and work.

It took a minor revolution in Israeli culture to bring Dvora

Baron back to the Hebrew reading public, a revolution signaled and aided by Nurit Govrin's rediscovery and publication in 1988 of Baron's early uncollected stories in Hebrew and Yiddish and by Amia Lieblich's publication, in 1991, of a biography of the author (issued in English translation in 1997 as *Conversations with Dvora: An Experimental Biography of the First Modern Hebrew Woman Writer,* the companion to this volume). Given the fervently Hebraist scene in which Baron wrote, it is not surprising that Baron's early Yiddish stories were not generally known before the appearance of Govrin's book. The renewed interest in Baron is part of a larger cultural shift, marked by a growing appreciation for Yiddish and the Eastern European past; in this context, Baron's literary world embodies a dimension of diasporic Judaism to which Israeli culture has only recently become more open. In an age when feminism has made some inroads, Baron's work can be valued for presenting the shtetl world from a perspective to which Hebrew and Yiddish literature rarely gave voice before—that of the Jewish woman, and of other disenfranchised members of the community. Baron's stories also reveal the author as a self-conscious participant in international modernism, continually experimenting with shifts in voice and perspective and inventing a complex expressive syntax in the service of her art. It is the modernist, feminist Dvora Baron that this translation has attempted to introduce to an English-speaking audience.

Dvora Baron was born in 1887, in the small Lithuanian town of Ouzda, where her father was serving as rabbi. She was her father's favorite, and he personally educated her. She left home at the age of fifteen—with her parents' blessing!—to acquire a secular education in Minsk and Kovno, working as a tutor and establishing her reputation as a Hebrew and Yiddish writer. Whereas a number of women had overcome the odds and written in Hebrew before her, Baron was the first woman to make a career for herself as a Hebrew writer. In 1910, after her father died, her shtetl was destroyed in a pogrom, and her long engagement to the Hebrew writer Moshe Ben Eliezer ended, she immigrated to Palestine. There she met and married Yosef Aharonovich, a prominent Zionist activist and the editor-in-chief of *The Young Worker,* where Baron also held a position on the editorial staff. Shortly after their daughter's birth in 1914, Yosef and Dvora were exiled to Egypt by the Ottoman authorities along with hundreds of others and allowed to return to Palestine only at the end of World War I. In 1922, both of them resigned their positions at the magazine and Baron began her long seclusion from the larger world, cared for by her daughter until her death. In her last thirty-three years, she did not set foot outside her apartment, not even to attend her husband's 1937 funeral. Tsipora, who never married or had children, died in 1971.

If Baron was exceptional, it was, first of all, in being the child of a rabbi who defied convention when it came to educating his gifted daughter. Girls in Baron's milieu were kept from acquiring an education in Hebrew texts, the core of a traditional Jewish education. At most, they were taught to read the Hebrew alphabet (which was also used to write Yiddish); the Jewish woman's library was limited to Yiddish Bible translations and prayer books. Baron's father, however, ensured that his daughter would learn the biblical and rabbinic sources, allowing Dvora to attend the classes he held in the town synagogue for boys while she sat behind the partition in the "women's section." Acquiring a traditional education, it should be noted, was the only way to become a Hebrew writer in Baron's day, when Hebrew had not yet become a vernacular. Baron's work, with its dense layers of allusion, demonstrates how thoroughly she absorbed these sources. Nevertheless, the fact that she had been given only qualified access to the community of scholars complicated her place in the world of Hebrew letters: sitting alone in the women's section, she was physically and intellectually isolated from the worlds of both women and men.

However remarkable the image of the young girl studying Torah behind the partition, it never found direct expression in Baron's stories. The closest the writer came to describing that experience is perhaps in "Deserted Wife," the last section of which describes a preacher's sermon from the perspective of an uneducated woman sitting behind the synagogue partition; the story makes an implicit case for the power of a woman's "misunderstanding" of rabbinic discourse, of her literalism in understanding the sermon's allegorical description of Israel as God's abandoned bride. Indirectly, though, Baron's curious position on both sides of the synagogue divide shapes her work everywhere. She uses an erudite, incisive Hebrew prose to portray characters whose class and gender would never have allowed them access to the knowledge she had (or the social status it conferred). Her early, uncollected Hebrew and Yiddish stories are particularly forthright in their critique of traditional Jewish culture: "Sister," for instance, is a bitter indictment of a family's disappointment over the birth of yet another daughter. Some of Baron's concerns seem remarkably contemporary: "Kaddish," first published in a Hebrew version in 1908 and in Yiddish two years later, involves a young girl's determination to say kaddish for her grandfather, a ritual reserved for male off-spring; this very struggle later came to occupy the center of American Jewish feminist activism. "Burying the Books" trans-poses the struggle for gender equality to the sexually segregated world of the Jewish sources; the young narrator fights to have her mother's damaged *tkhine,* a Yiddish prayer collection for women, ritually buried alongside the damaged Hebrew books.

Baron may have felt that some of these early stories were too nakedly angry; in any case, she resisted including them in the various collections she published beginning in 1927, calling them "rags" (the very term of denigration used against the mother's *tkhine* that "Burying the Books" criticizes). Themes from the early stories sometimes resurface in the later collection; but while Baron's critical voice tends to be muted in this later work, her subversive wit still comes across, if more subtly and ironically. It is now the structure of the stories, their allusions and shifts in perspective, that carry the critical force, rather than direct pronouncements by the narrator or characters. "In the Beginning," for instance, by echoing Genesis (in Hebrew, the biblical book is called "In the Beginning," after its first word) makes the largest possible claim for its author's ambition: to do no less than reimagine the Bible, this time with a woman at center stage. The allusion goes further than the title: "In the Beginning" echoes the double creation narrative in Genesis— the narrator begins her story by describing the first horrified reaction of the urbane rebbetzin, the rabbi's wife, to the squalid shtetl in which she will be living and then stops herself short to begin the story again, "in a more appropriate version," by talking about the crucial event, the arrival of the new rabbi, with the wife now kept properly in the background. We hope it is not too far-fetched to suggest that the truncated opening might echo the self-censorship that directly preceded the publication of this story.

It would be reductive to see Baron's stories, even the early ones, as motivated solely by a feminist or, more generally, by an ideological critique of traditional Jewish society. She is, first of all, a prose writer of many styles. Baron has been credited with refining modern Hebrew literature through the exquisitely detailed realism typical of her later, better-known work. Largely overlooked have been her early stories, in which high-modernist surrealism combines with an artful manipulation of such popular genres as the gothic and the fairy tale to explore the psychosexual depths of human relations in a traditional culture. A story like "Kaddish," for instance, cannot be reduced to a battle cry for women's right to memorialize their dead: rebellion and pious love are curiously intermingled in the girl's mourning, and the suggestion of incestuous attraction between the girl and her grandfather further complicates the matter. The story ultimately invokes the tensions inherent in the relations between the sexes, the generations, even the living and the dead. Elsewhere, Baron pioneers a sexual (rather than historical or economic) exploration of Jewish-gentile relations, in the case of "Liska," through the figure of a "Jewish" dog.

Perhaps Baron is most appreciated today for her ability to present without sentimentality a world that no longer exists, in all of its singularity and nuance. In Baron's stories, place acquires the weight and dimensions of plot and character. Her work shows us a shtetl that is class-ridden and full of human complications, a shtetl that includes the gentile street (often obscured in other Jewish writings)—Baron never succumbs to the nostalgic fantasy of a lost unity, the form in which many American readers will have encountered this world. What we experience in these stories is not a composite portrait of life in Jewish Eastern Europe but rather the materiality of a single remote Lithuanian town, the smell of each season, the texture of fur jackets and tattered caftans, of rough bark and steaming hot potatoes. The shtetl, in these stories, emerges anew with its intricacy and tensions intact.

This book presents eighteen (a felicitous Jewish number) of the eighty or so stories Baron published in her lifetime. Nine of these are from the earlier work, and another nine from the later, post-1927 collections. The first section presents the better-known, "mature" Baron, starting in quasi-biblical order with "In the Beginning" and "The First Day." The second section of the book presents the best of her early work; our placing them after the later stories reflects Baron's own sense that her early writing was marginal to her work as a whole. These stories are important not only for their historical value, as artifacts of a radical young writer or evidence of early talent; some of these stories are as well crafted and powerful as anything in Baron's collections, and many of them, moreover, attest to the writer's stylistic affiliations with the early modernist prose of this century. Most of the stories in both sections come from her Hebrew corpus; in three instances we translated a Yiddish story, or a Yiddish version of a story that also has a Hebrew version (noting the Yiddish original at the end of the story). Where versions of stories exist in both languages, on rare occasions we took the liberty of choosing an apt phrase from the version in the alternative language.

Dvora Baron's style is both fluid and intricate, pushing the flexibility of Hebrew or Yiddish syntax to its very limits. Her stylistic toolbox is enormous, ranging from virtuoso passages that capture the shifting movement of the eye or the disturbances of a half-conscious mind to the rough rhythms of colloquial speech. Baron's work, early and late, is also highly allusive, reflecting the author's profound knowledge of both biblical and rabbinic literature. This allusiveness operates on the broadest levels (entire short-story collections echoing Genesis, for instance) and in specific words and phrases, often to ironic, or even iconoclastic, effect. Baron uses mock-epic allusion, for instance, to describe the gentile postman of a village abandoned by all its Jewish men as the shtetl's King Saul, "towering head and shoulders above the crowd" of Jewish women. Hebrew sources are, of course, the basic material for Baron's writing, as they were for her peers, but there is nothing automatic or "learned" about Baron's gestures toward these texts: Baron's characters live both very close to the Bible and at a sometimes comic distance from it. There are moments when her narrator comments on the two worlds her characters inhabit: "In the Beginning" juxtaposes the parched heat in the background of the weekly Torah portions with the muddy Eastern European autumn and frozen winter when these portions are being read, capturing both the proximity and distance between the Bible and those shtetl folk who live, unnaturally, by its refracted light.

Our major challenge in translating Baron was to capture the

impressionistic syntax, the reversals, interjections, and shifts and render them in idiomatic English prose. We also tried to register her allusiveness as often as possible, quoting from recent translations of the Bible, for their readability, combined, at times, with the King James version, for its usefulness in signaling the "biblical" flavor of the Hebrew to English readers. We kept the original Hebrew or Yiddish in the case of those words that might be familiar to the English reader; at the very least, these words help to signal the foreignness of the milieu Baron depicts. For readers unfamiliar with these terms, we have provided a brief glossary at the back of the book.

Because Baron's work is rich in ethnographic detail, we debated the question of footnotes, finally deciding that they would lend an academic air that belied the vibrancy of her writing. In the case of unfamiliar objects, customs, or rituals, of which Baron's work could fairly serve as a compendium, we either trusted the context to convey something of what was meant or inserted a short explanatory phrase in the text itself—unobtrusively, we hope. If these stories are nevertheless wondrous and strange, we would not have wished it otherwise.

Naomi Seidman
Chana Kronfeld

The Later Stories

In the Beginning

On the beginning of the new rebbetzin's life in Zhuzhikovka, the locals say:

She, the rebbetzin, was brought here a few years ago from some distant city in Poland.

There, in that city, the Polish one, her parents had a house made of polished stone, which was built like a kind of palace, with balconies and columns, and it was tall—ten Polish cubits high. They also had a garden to stroll in beside their house, and among the trees of this garden were flower beds and fountains, in which water rose up and spurted on its own, like the waters that flowed from the rock Moses smote. Was it any wonder, then, that when the rebbetzin arrived in Zhuzhikovka and took one look at the ruin of the community house and its desolate yard, she stopped in front of the door and decided that she wasn't going in?

She did go into the house, though, later on. She took off her hat, revealing a golden wig, a tumble of curls—and entered.

But after that, at night, when the welcoming reception had come to an end and the guests had gone off to their own houses, she sank in her city clothes onto the naked bench in the community hall and cried bitterly, while he, her young husband in his silk caftan, his rabbinic sash wound around his hips, stood beside her—at a loss.

This whole story should begin differently, in a more appropriate version—and here it is:

When the new rabbi was about to arrive and ascend to the rabbinic seat, the community president ordered that the streets be swept and the synagogue whitewashed just as if it were Passover or the High Holy Days. And since the guest was due to arrive at the station on Friday afternoon, the shtetl folk changed their usual practice and made sure to heat the bathhouse on Thursday before sundown.

That night every stove and oven in every house was stoked. And the women cooked and baked and shampooed their children's hair and made sure to darn their tattered clothing, so that no shame would come upon the community as they waited at the station to greet the newcomer.

Early the next morning, just as the sun emerged from behind the synagogue roof, the entire community set out with its women and children, fanning out along the paths that led to the train station.

It certainly was a sight, this crowd of Jews in their colorful rags, threading their way across the wide fields at such an early hour. The farmer women, crouching over their vegetable beds, straightened up in amazement, shielding their eyes with their hands to stare long and hard after this motley crew.

When the crowd arrived at the village of Kaminka, not without some trepidation they skirted the pasture, where the dogs roamed as freely as the cattle. There was still a stubble field to cross after that, with the overgrown thorns scratching their legs, especially those who were barefoot.

But here, at last, appeared the station, a garish clapboard building with its windows sealed shut and its dusty copper basin by the entrance, the corroded dipper hanging from a chain over it. A bell rang, wheels clattered and roared, and two men, pillars of the community, came pushing through the crowd toward the rumbling train that had come to a halt, the new woolen sleeves glinting with strange innocence on their old Sabbath caftans—and they presented the young rabbi with his writ of appointment.

Yes, it's true, all those men had new sleeves sewn into their caftans, but these new sleeves only made the drabness of their threadbare outfits stand out more starkly, and the young rebbetzin, leaning with charming urbanity on her parasol, rubbed her eyes as if in shock, scarcely able to believe what she was seeing.

But now a trumpet blast shook the air. And then a drumbeat and a fife were heard, and the procession moved: the young rabbi in his silk caftan at its center, with the congregation leaders at his right and left, and around them the rabble, merry shouts, and a cloud of dust, and inside the carriage that lumbered behind—the rebbetzin, suede gloves on her hands, the ostrich feather in her hat nodding to the rhythm of the swaying carriage.

Along the roadside: groves of trees, haystacks at the edges of fields, flocks of sheep with their dogs herding them, and before the rebbetzin's eyes finally appeared the shtetl, with its poor huddled houses propped up on their poles, the forsaken wooden hoist suspended over the mouth of the well, and the windmill with its sluggish arms sagging listlessly by the mountainous garbage dump.

From here, atop the straw seat inside the carriage, it was also impossible not to notice the narrow wooden racks attached to the cornices and suspended from the beams of every house, and the blocks of cheese drying on them were so perfectly triangular that it was hard to believe that they had been made by hand and not some sort of machine.

And soon enough the "community house" itself came into view, a small building propped up, like the others, on poles, and on the heap of garbage in the yard—would you believe?— stood a milk goat, a white goat with innocent eyes, who, noticing the carriage stop beside the house, approached and grabbed a mouthful of straw from the underside of the rebbetzin's seat, and then stood and chewed it with goatish seriousness.

And now is when the story they tell about the rebbetzin refusing to enter the community house took place.

The old woman, Sarah Riva, who had been hired as a housekeeper even before the new owners arrived, afterward described in detail how she, the rebbetzin, threw herself down in all her finery on the community bench and sobbed, while he, her rabbi husband, dressed in silk, paced the room—in consternation.

When it came to the point where she, the rebbetzin, raising her head and looking at him through a flood of tears, mentioned that strange creature, the goat—he could no longer hold back his laughter, pausing for a minute at the bench to stand beside her.

"Well, the truth is that you're just an inexperienced little goat yourself," he said.

Long and perplexing days followed, late-summer days in a remote Lithuanian shtetl. The silk-embroidered tablecloths, which were taken out of the bridal chest every once in a while, only heightened the poverty of the room when they were spread out over the tables. The curtains turned out to be much too wide and long for the windows, and the rebbetzin, after unsuccessfully trying a few times to make them fit, was forced to return them to the chest.

Nevertheless, these were bright summer days, and in the morning, when she opened the shutters, the radiant sunshine that flooded everything amazed her. And if on one side it illuminated only the dusty, gloomy alley, with its unpainted houses, on the other side the eye was transfixed by the meadow, a wide green meadow, over which stretched a sky at least as deep and blue as the city sky back in Poland.

This was a bustling hour in the alley and around it. At the well, the water carriers came and went with their buckets. Women gave the goats their morning milking by their front doors and little boys, with fringed garments over their short pants, streamed with their books to the cheders.

Very soon, from the end of the alley, their voices rang out and continued throughout the day, voices sweeter and clearer than any she, the rebbetzin, had ever heard.

The young rabbi, noticing how she stood listening to those voices, once asked her whether she had seen the charity boxes in these poor houses yet. And, indeed, in the very same spot where the racks for the cheese were attached to the outside of the houses could be found, on the other side of the wall inside nearly every house, a whole shelf full of tin cans, with the acronyms of all the yeshivas in the world inscribed on their rounded sides. Precisely how coins were deposited into these cans was captured, to the consternation of the locals, by a roving photographer who came through here once on a Friday afternoon.

He, the stranger, standing at the threshold of his inn as the sun was setting, was fascinated to see the landlady take some copper coins out of a special pouch and arrange them on the tabletop, from which she had folded the tablecloth back for that purpose. The house had been straightened up and scrubbed. At the head of the table, under a satin Sabbath cloth, lay two loaves of challah while across from them, at the other end of the table, the candles stood ready in their candlesticks for lighting, and she, the woman, sweeping the coins into her hand and raising her youngest child in her arms toward the charity boxes, was handing him the coins to toss into the slots, when now, suddenly, turning her head, she caught sight of the "case" in the visitor's hands and saw what he was doing to her and to her son, and she collapsed onto the bench before her and burst into tears.

Yes, these Zhuzhikovkans were a strange bunch—the rebbetzin shook her head as she listened to the stories people told her, though her face no longer darkened to hear these things as in the beginning.

She was peaceful and content even after that, when the autumn came, and the mud closed in on the shtetl from every side.

Now the meadow lay yellowish and withering on the other

side of the windows, while the goats wandered up and down the alley with sagging bellies and sparse coats, bleating pitifully. How terrifying was the sight of the shadowy shops, with their flimsy signs hanging by a thread, and the barrels of annihilated and frozen Dutch herring, from whose round, wide-open eyes, despair itself now peered out.

Beside the well in the market square, in the middle of the day, the carriage drivers could be seen trudging along, sodden, behind their unharnessed horses, and limply pulling the slippery water hoist.

Desolate lay the roads of the town, desolate.

In the early mornings, the women no longer went outside to lay out wedges of cheese to dry, and if a woman appeared on the expanse of mud, it was some courageous mother slogging along, in men's boots, carrying her children to their cheder.

These were hard, hard days in the remote shtetl.

The young rebbetzin, if she heard the goat bleating, would go out in her plush coat and tenderly offer her a little straw from the dilapidated roof.

At night the wind blew, wrestling with the roof and ripping off the new patches of thatched straw. Far away, somewhere outside the town, dogs barked and their brethren on the gentile street responded with long wails. And the young rebbetzin, waking from sleep with fragments of dreams still caught between her eyelids—distant dreams with the afterimage of city lights—would gaze out into the darkness of her poor home, frightened and amazed at what she would see when she awoke, though she was no longer as despondent as in the early days. For together with the howl of the wind outside the windows she could also hear the voice of the rabbi, who sat at the table by lamplight, reading, chanting, and singing. And if sometimes a tear rolled down her face, it was only a consoling tear, brought forth by the sound of the mournful singing.

Once, on a night like this, the rabbi sat at the head of the table, rehearsing aloud the sermon he would be giving on the weekly Torah portion, the chapter "And Jacob left." He spun and wove together the various themes with ease, illuminating each of them in the refined light of his mind, pronouncing every word, as usual, as clearly and distinctly as if he were counting coins. This happened at the beginning of the month of Kislev, perhaps the most forbidding season of the year. The rain, which poured all day and all night, had flooded even the last of the dry footpaths alongside the roads and fields. There was no more bread to be had in the shtetl—and the young rabbi, sitting at his desk, delved ever more deeply into Jacob's leave-taking of Beersheba, how the sun had set upon him as he made his way through a field, and how, as he lay lonesome and lost, a stone for his pillow, on that very first night of exile God showed him the marvelous ladder, the one whose feet stood on the ground and whose head reached to the very heavens.

"Behold, I am with you, and shall keep you," the rabbi sang God's promise, weaving together more and more strands of the tapestry of his sermon, strengthening it from time to time with further prooftexts from various places.

For while the verses of the Torah portion served him as the foundation and building blocks, the words of the Prophets and later Writings were the mortar and ornamental detail.

Thus, for example, when he reached the place where it was recounted how Jacob met our Mother Rachel and how he rolled the heavy boulder from the well, he brought in the verse from the Songs of Songs, that "Many waters cannot quench love, neither can the floods drown it."

By and by he came, also, to the passage of Rachel's longing for children, and from that to how the Lord remembered her, listening to her and granting her a son:

"Enlarge the place of your tent, for you shall break forth out on the right hand and on the left," the rabbi rose from his seat and paced the length of the room, trilling his words in a mournful and tender tone—so mournful and tender that the rebbetzin on the other side of the partition couldn't stop herself from standing up and holding her arms out toward the room.

Is there any need to describe the things that passed between those two in the still of the night, in the raging heart of autumn? In any case there's no way of knowing all the details, since the old housekeeper had set up her bed that night in the kitchen, at the far end of the other room. What is clear is that the rabbi, who was now standing beside his wife, no longer called her "little fool" or referred to her as an inexperienced young goat, as he once had. He just soothed her with kind words, hinting to her about the child that she too would soon embrace, like the matriarch Rachel in her day, and he stayed with her until she had calmed down.

Autumn in the shtetl was meanwhile coming to an end and in its place came winter, white, aggressive, and brilliant, and changed everything all at once.

In the weekly Torah portions, though, the story continued to be as parched, summery, and wearisome as before.

Pharaoh still saw in his dream the cows on the banks of the Nile. In the Land of Canaan there was famine, bread could not be found anywhere and starvation lay heavy and oppressive, while here in Zhuzhikovka the snow fell and covered the fields and roads, and the rebbetzin, when she found a windowpane free of frost, gazed serenely at the winter sleighs that slid along toward the shtetl, laden with an abundance of food.

Birch wood, brought straight from the forest, caught fire at the entrance to the stove as soon as it was lit, without any kindling or additional help. At daybreak, the smoke rose from the chimneys toward the sky in a straight line, unwavering. American potatoes, substantial and heavy, were peeled, breaking into floury, appetizing fissures as soon as they came to a boil, and over the well at the end of the alley the hoist with its bucket squeaked powerfully and diligently.

Days of plenty had come to the town and among those who came to the market square were Jews from the far reaches of the surrounding country, able-bodied villagers wearing farmers' hoods, and when they swung their heavy fur coats with their thick collars, they gave off an aroma foreign to the town air, the smoky scent of resin ovens and the pine forests that stretched to the Polesian marshes and beyond.

One of these villagers, who came for his first visit to the new rabbi, brought, in addition to a bag of chickpeas, a large fatted goose with white feathers, who, as soon as the housekeeper loosened the rope around his legs, immediately stuck his neck into the chicken coop and gobbled up the hen's feed with the calm self-assurance common only among those fat creatures who have no concern for anyone else's property.

"Serve him up with those," the man gestured with the tip of his whip toward the sack of chickpeas.

Although old Sarah Riva had decided that these peas should

be set aside for some other time—a time of celebration and
"Mazel tov"—she nodded good-naturedly. And later that evening the rebbetzin, as she sat by the lamp and passed her hand
over those chickpeas, cool and smooth, felt a shiver run through
her, sweeter than any she had ever felt.

Within the next few weeks lambs, tender and newly weaned,
also began to arrive from the surrounding farms, and the first
of the dairy products.

The cheese, which was brought in capacious earthen farm
jugs, was sometimes covered with a fine layer of frost that
crackled lightly when it was removed. In order to knead it into
rounds, first the cheese had to be brought close to the oven to
soften and thaw, and then a special fragrance would suffuse the
house, signaling the approach of spring.

Easily, as on a winter's sleigh, the days now slid by. Among
those who arrived at the railroad station, finally, were the em-
issaries from the yeshivas, men with noble beards dressed in
rabbinic caftans, who, with their special hammers, without a
speck of rust, pulled the charity boxes off the wall with amazing
efficiency, and as they arranged the coins in rows on the table,
the narrow rectangle where the cans had been nailed stood pale
and waiting, as if ashamed of its nakedness.

And in the weekly Torah portion, meanwhile, Pharaoh's stubbornness and his refusal to let the Israelites go out of Egypt
ended. The plagues came—incessant, harsh, and surprisingly
inventive.

After the three days of darkness came the final blow, the
decisive one—the plague of the firstborn. And the rout was
complete:

Moses and Aaron were called to Pharaoh in the middle of the night, and the Israelites were compelled to leave in a frenzy, even before their dough had risen.

As they camped for a moment on the verge of freedom, before Baal-Zephon, another unpleasant little incident intervened:

The Israelites lifted their eyes and behold—Egypt was riding in pursuit. But salvation came in the blink of an eye: the waters were split and the sea became dry ground before those being pursued, and the finest of Pharaoh's horsemen were hurled into the deep, and the Israelites walked out with their heads held high.

It was the Sabbath when the Song of the Sea was read in the shtetl. On the windowpanes of the synagogue the ice had melted in the course of the service, and the rays of sunlight streaming through them fell across the wooden lions that crouched like two kindly steers at the top of the Holy Ark, beside the velvet curtain.

The Song of Deborah was also read:

They that are delivered from the noise of archers in the places of drawing water, there shall they rehearse the righteous acts of the Lord. They fought from heaven, the stars in their courses fought against Sisera, and during lunch, when the door was opened so that crumbs could be thrown to the birds, the sound of their chirping burst into the house and spread a new spirit all around, the breath of spring, which although it tarried, speedily would come.

The approach of spring was also soon prophesied by the new wooden vessels that were brought from the villages to be sold.

The beets were brought up from the cellar. The women, in

their clean cotton aprons, came with the first of their questions about the laws of Passover and, while the rabbi sat at the head of the table, looking into his book, the women couldn't take their eyes off the rebbetzin, who now—she had slimmed down after the birth and looked even taller—had become so beautiful. Once, on a day like this, the rebbetzin went out to the front yard, a thin sanded board in her hand.

Outside the roofs dripped merrily. Behind the garden gates the newborn chicks clucked musically, with clear, abrupt cries— like spring, and the rebbetzin, lifting the board high, marked the place on the wall for the rack where the cheese wedges would dry in the summer, and she hammered in the nails with her own hand.

The sound of the hammer woke the newborn, who was lying in her cradle, and she let out a kind of coo, which sounded very much like the murmur of the spring waters rushing down the foot of the nearby slope. The rebbetzin, when the sound reached her, hurried back to the community room, went over to the cradle and looked down at the baby, and a smile appeared on her lips that slowly illuminated her entire face—that smile was the very first thing that each of us children of the rabbi of Zhuzhikovka saw the moment we emerged into the light of day.

The First Day

At around the same time that my mother, the rebbetzin of a town poor in deeds, gave birth to me, the landlady of the estate, that forceful woman, gave birth to her first son, who also turned out to be her only child. This little gentleman would become a thorn in my side more than once in my journey through life.

The very first time we met—it was a summery Sabbath afternoon and I was a frail little girl, making my way with the last of my strength through the pine forest next to the estate— he set the courtyard dogs on me from behind the gate.

The sound of my shrieks must have been chilling as I stumbled between the dank and impenetrable walls, because both from the main gate and from the nearby gardens the servant boys came running, hushing the dogs as they ran; and then, as I leaned against the gate, which would have been beyond my powers to climb, I saw him, a son of the gentry, standing there in his silk ankle socks, his shaved head bare and a flash of malice on his well-fed face—and I hated him.

But all that happened later on and will perhaps be described in detail somewhere else. This time I just wanted to tell the story of what happened to me on the first day of my life, a short, meaningless winter day with low and utterly dispiriting clouds in the sky over my shtetl.

At twilight of the previous day the estate carriage, which had come to pick up my father to be the godfather at the circumcision to be held the following morning, had already stopped before our house.

The harness bell, whose ring tinkled very pleasantly in the stillness of the dusk, made the most hideous impression on my paternal grandmother, the rebbetzin of Tokhanovka, who was visiting us now.

She looked at the gentile coachman practically with abhorrence when, entering, covered with snow, his whip under his armpit, he announced that he had no foot blanket with him in the carriage since the lady had apparently forgotten to provide one.

"We can find a blanket ourselves, it hasn't come to that yet," she wanted to make sure he informed the young lady, who was, unfortunately, her cousin and one of the family—against her will, but there it was, she was in fact a member of the Tokhanovkan family, and there was nothing that could be done about it.

Actually, the matter was much more complicated than you might think. Years ago she, the aforementioned landlady, had turned down a proposal to marry the man who would later hold the position of rabbi of Zhuzhikovka, that is, my father.

The matchmaker, who had traveled the entire distance between Tokhanovka and Zhuzhikovka by foot, crossing the river

twice in the process, returned in a few days' time with an ab-
solute refusal, bringing with him for his efforts a single ruble
and an almost new woolen coat, which was the disgrace of the
entire family for a long time afterward.

All this I heard years later from my sister, who also told me
a few other things about the past, which was as interesting to
me as it was to her.

That same evening, when my father had left for the estate
and a dim pewter lamp, hesitant and wavering, had been lit at
the corner of the stove, a silence settled in the house that was
not broken again for the rest of that evening.

A workaday supper, with just the women's grace after meals
at its conclusion, was eaten at the end of the table on a tablecloth
folded in two—and the rebbetzin from Tokhanovka, taking
off her distinguished fringed headdress, for which she could
find a place of honor among the poor furnishings only after an
assiduous search, extinguished the lamp with one vigorous and
ill-tempered breath, and by the creaking of the bed, which
shook beneath her as she lay down, one could guess that the
image of her cousin's house on the estate outside town rose
before her eyes with perfect clarity:

The plush embroidered ballroom chairs arranged regally on
the carpet, the silver chandelier glittering overhead with all the
colors of its crystals, the brass pots shining in the kitchen across
from the blazing oven and the warm honey dumplings, which
the lady would roll flat with her rolling pin, the abundant
strings of pearls around her neck quivering with every movement.

In short, is there any dearth of visions that might pass before
the eyes of a rebbetzin, lying in the room of the practically

destitute daughter-in-law she did not love and reciting her bedtime prayers?

In about three hours, after the lamp had been lit once
more—and then extinguished again—and the flurry of activity
incited by my birth had ceased, a silence arose in the house
stranger than any I had ever known in any world.

Oh, this first night in the house of my ancestors, deep in the
harsh winter, when the oven had been stoked so stingily and
the flame of the lamp had no confidence in its own power.

Between the sixth and seventh hour, when, from somewhere,
a few pale and sickly rays of morning light managed to penetrate, I was able to see in some detail the backside of the stove,
which rose naked and exposed across from my cradle, and
whose sad and naked chimney, also without plaster, gazed
hopelessly toward the empty space into which it leaned—but
did not fall.

Amazing and touching as well was the rusty and crooked
screw that stuck out of the rafter above me, and which, in its
enormous solitude in the wide expanse of the ceiling, unemployed, purposeless (though obviously someone must have
screwed it in there once), was for many years a symbol for me
of everything unhappy and superfluous in this life.

But most amazing was the squeak of the felt shoes that
reached me from the other side of the wooden partition, and
which grew increasingly cross as the day brightened.

What's the point of beating around the bush? In short, my
paternal grandmother, the rebbetzin of Tokhanovka, who was
now visiting our house, was dissatisfied with my entry into the
light of this world.

Girls, she said, she already had enough of from her daughter-in-law the rebbetzin of Khmilovka and also from the other daughter-in-law, the rebbetzin of Borisovka, and she had reached her limit, she said, with these girls. This wasn't the reason she had left her yeast business and her house in Tokhanovka and come to sit around her son's house in Zhuzhikovka—and in general: "Now what were they going to say in the courtyard?"

It's embarrassing to relate, but the events should be written simply, exactly as they happened: at an early hour of the morning, just when it had become light enough to write, she sent for the neighbor boy, the bookbinder's son, and recited to him the things he should write in her name to her husband, the rabbi of Tokhanovka.

In place of the distinguished headdress, the one with the fringes, a woolen kerchief now covered her head, tied under her chin with an aggressive, almost menacing knot.

All the eternal hatred of an aged mother-in-law for her young daughter-in-law was concentrated in her glasses, which peered down at the table to see whether everything had been properly written with regard to her bad luck in the matter of her sons' matches. And when the boy, embarrassed, finally got to his feet, in their oversized men's boots, and tried to escape— she ran after him with the sheet of paper in her hand, her glasses slipping unchecked off her face.

At approximately ten o'clock, as the chill in the house deepened and the oven remained unlit, a conversation like this one could be heard between the two rebbetzins, from their opposite sides of the partition:

"Mother-in-law," sighed the rebbetzin of Zhuzhikovka, "the baby has to be given some sugar water."

"Sugar water?" shuddered the rebbetzin of Tokhanovka.

"Why yes, sugar water," the voice of the rebbetzin of Zhu-zhikovka fell, "and also she should be covered with another robe, so she doesn't catch cold."

"Did you hear that? Big deal, so she'll catch cold," squeaked the rebbetzin of Tokhanovka in her felt shoes, gathering the various pastries that had been prepared for the circumcision to return them to the bakery.

Absolutely, she looked just like a tigress, sweeping around the room like that in her wide-striped apron.

Having spent her life in the vicinity of learned men, listening to their conversations, my grandmother also knew some sayings from the discourse of our sages in the matter of a daughter and her value in life. Thus, for example, she knew that if the son is compared to wine, then the daughter is nothing but vinegar; if a son is as wheat, then the daughter is like barley. True: there is a need for wine and a need for vinegar, but the need for wine is greater than for vinegar; so too, one needs both wheat and barley but—the need for wheat is greater than that for barley.

The erudition of this old rebbetzin was awesome. Like giant boulders the sayings rolled from her mouth, one heavier and more frightening than the next—and the rebbetzin of Zhu-zhikovka lay on the other side of the partition with her white childbirth kerchief around her head, pale, shaken, with not a word to say in response.

In her brain, exhausted after the sleepless night, neverthe-less wandered fragments of thoughts and arguments, which some other time she might have been able to seize upon in her own defense. After all, it would be enough to bring up the day her first daughter had been born, when her husband, the rabbi, reading aloud from the letter he had written to his father, explained to her explicitly that what was meant by the verse "And God blessed Abraham in everything" was no less than that God had given Abraham a daughter whose name was "Everything."

In fact, there was no doubt that if he, her husband, were here now, he would find in his kind heart something similar to say regarding this daughter, the second one, as well—the young rebbetzin sighed, raising her head to the window and seeing that the sky was already darkening and he, the rabbi, had still not returned.

The short winter day passed, in the meantime, and approached its end. The shadows, rising and falling in turn, lapped slowly against the slats of the cradle, the wooden partition, and the mother's bed beside it.

When things had finally reached the point that even the stove and its chimney lay in deep gloom, forming a frightening, towering mass across from me, I tried in my anguish to roll around and shake myself free of my prison, but I had been swaddled, alas, by a tyrant's hands, the old woman's hands, and so, twisting my head back and forth and seeing that only darkness and silence enveloped me, I did the one thing that any person would do if they were miserable and lonely and salvation was distant: I raised my voice—and I wept.

And suddenly, a miracle (later I was informed that all rescues, by their very nature, arrive suddenly and miraculously): from out of the darkness all around, far from the house, a sort of tinkling sound could be heard, and before anyone could get to the window, the door rejoiced in being opened and into the house stepped a man who—I knew, although I had never met him before—would be dearer to me in the course of time than all life's pleasures.

With the swinging of his sheepskin coat as he took it off, a special smell, a delicious smell that could only belong to Father, had already wafted toward me, but when he came over to the wooden partition, drew the two half-curtains apart and called in his clear voice "Mazel tov"—I caught my breath in excitement and within a split second had hushed right down.

Is it necessary to go on and tell what happened next? After that the lamps were lit on both sides of the partition, my side and the other, and warmth and well-being spread through the house.

With a ringing sweeter than anything I had ever heard, the silverware clattered onto the tablecloth as the table was set, and a smell pervaded the air, the smell of the evening's dish that had been hidden in the oven since morning and which they know how to make only in Zhuzhikovka, Lithuania.

My father, who was walking back and forth across the room and asking about the progression of the day's events, was very sorry when Mother told him that the letter to his old father had already been written that morning without him. He stood beside my mother's bed with a radiant face and his hands tucked under his rabbinic sash (no doubt exactly as he had stood four years earlier, the day my older sister was born), and lectured to her on the contents of the letter that ought to have been written to his father, telling her, in the course of the lecture, about what had happened to Rabbi Simeon Bar-Ami, on the day his daughter was born, when he met the Babylonian, the great Rabbi Hiya, who said that now the Holy One, blessed be He, had truly begun to bless him . . .

"Those were his words, his exact words," he stressed with his clear voice, watching as my mother's cheeks grew rosy and her eyes misted over.

As for my grandmother, the same thing happened to her that happens to an ice floe when it is suddenly struck by the rays of the sun.

At the sight of her son's glowing face, the angry creases in her forehead smoothed themselves out and the knot underneath her chin moved and noticeably loosened. And when my father finally turned to her and said that the son who had been born there, on the estate, had been given a family name and was to be called after the uncle from Tokhanovka, Reb Shmulik of blessed memory—her kerchief came undone all at once and its two ends remained untied for the duration of that evening.

The water splashed under her hands with a completely different music now as she scrubbed the earthenware dishes, and this time, the bowls were displayed on the shelf in a neat row, face-down, as if they were burnished brass.

Her train of thought went something like this:

If over there they named the boy after the uncle, of blessed memory, Reb Shmulik, then it would only be proper that here they should name the girl after the aunt, may she rest in peace, Hodl, and God willing—they'll be the ones who come begging to us, and then we'll be the ones to decline—she sank, in the glow of revenge, onto her bed, after having exchanged her woolen kerchief for a white night-kerchief, and the murmured bedtime prayer, which had ceased for a whole minute, flowed peacefully and quietly again like a stream in the wake of a storm.

For a long time my father continued to walk back and forth

on the other side of the partition, singing to himself an offhand, casual tune, the sort of tune that might be sung to soothe some-one or put them to sleep, and which flows easily and fluently from every father's lips. His own tune, the extraordinary one, the one which in the course of the years, during those nights in my bed, would mix with my sadness like blended wine, came afterward, a few hours later, as he sat over his books at the table by the light of the lamp, no longer pondering the fate of sons or daughters on this earth but rather that of humanity in gen-eral.

Reproachful, piercing, laced with gentleness—as if with a magical wand he lifted the veil from my future for an instant, and I peeked: gloom and grayness, with no passage or exit, like those stone walls between which I reeled years later, chased by the hand of an invisible oppressor, between the very fangs of dogs—and I was shaken.

At the sound of my cries Father came from the other side of the partition and rocked me, going back, in an instant, to the tune from before, the offhand one, the one every father knows by heart.

"There, there, it's nothing, it's nothing," he soothed me, soothed me and sang, until I indeed calmed down and, ex-hausted—fell asleep. So ended the first day of my life.

Fradl

Charming but sad was the woman Fradl in Chana's shtetl, whom fate had dealt with harshly and she struggled long and hard against it.

She was the daughter of one of the best of the local families and she had a large house in the community alley that she had inherited from her parents, who had died when she was young, and her relatives who had raised her were the ones who, when the time came, found her a mate—an educated boy from the next town who was also of good family. And the two were engaged and the dowry remitted, and after the wedding they came to live in the big house that was in the community alley.

A few elegant pieces of furniture were brought from the provincial capital, and the woman also had clothes made up in the big-city style, and in them she walked from room to spacious room, in which reigned order and cleanliness and a frozen stillness.

The lacy curtains here bestowed a pale light, something like the afterimage of snow, and even the silver bowls in the cupboard glinted with a frosty whitish shine, and the woman, as she gazed out every once in a while at the alley, which was darkened by poverty but radiated the joy of life, seemed as if she were warming herself in that radiance.

A school for the children of the poor had been founded at that time, and her husband—Avraham-Noach was his name—volunteered to teach arithmetic there. Aside from that he also had some business, commercial matters, which he had taken up at that time, and he spent most of the hours of his day buying and selling. And when he came home for the meal, he would look into the newspaper or some book, an activity best done quietly. And so nothing could be heard here other than the clink of silverware and china as they ate. Afterward the tablecloth was carefully shaken off and the woman went off somewhere, to her embroidery, or else she stepped out at dusk to the bench beside her house and sat here, her kerchief bound modestly around her head, a young woman of charm and goodness, but without that secret joy one sees in a woman's face in the first flush of married love. And when the neighbor women around noticed this, their hearts went out to her, but the rebbetzin, an intelligent woman, said:

"She is still 'empty,' which is why she is sad; when her hands are 'filled' she will find peace."

And it would be impossible not to mention here the widow Sarah-Leah and her son Chaim-Raphael, who also lived in that alley, and whose vegetable garden bordered on Fradl's yard.

They also had a spacious house, with a grassy yard where

wildflowers grew in abundance in the summertime. And Fradl, when she was young, had often come to play there. The kind-hearted Sarah-Leah had fed her sugar cookies with cherry jam and had embraced her tenderly, with a wistful sorrow, since she herself had not been blessed with a daughter. And her son Chaim-Raphael, already past his bar mitzvah then, had also attached himself to her, the little girl, during the hours he was out of school, swinging her in the swing in the corner of the garden, or pushing the doll carriage that had been brought for her from the city. He would loosen one of the screws and send the carriage flying down the paved path, while they, her little hand in his palm, ran after it laughing so brightly and merrily that even the mother, Sarah-Leah, would momentarily forget the sorrow of her widowhood at the sight and laugh right along with them.

And so the years passed and the little girl, who went off to live in her relatives' house after her parents died, became a young woman and went out for walks with Liebka, the daughter of her uncle Isser Levin, and with Reyzl, the daughter of her aunt Chana, and dressed as they did in skirts and cotton-knit shirts. And Chaim-Raphael also matured and grew tall and was already doing business with agents and landowners, since he, too, like his father, Yerucham-David, was in the grain trade.

Fradl he only saw from time to time—on the market square or in the linden avenue, and then he would incline his head to her politely, and while at such moments his cheeks would flush red with excitement, her face remained closed and cold.

And his friends, who saw into his heart, would go off with him on summer Sabbaths toward the Countess's wheat fields, where—they knew—the girl would be walking during those hours. But she, when they happened upon her on one of the trails, would flutter by as if she had not seen them; and the scent of her perfume, mingled with that of the field, would make the boy dizzy. And he finally decided in his own heart that he would no longer even set foot beyond the bounds of the town. And he also distanced himself from his friends, who had witnessed his weakness, and began to spend more time with the agents and dealers in the marketplace. From them he acquired a sharp and joking tongue—something a sensitive person wields, in most cases, only to hide a wounded heart—and on the Sabbath, while the Torah was being read in the synagogue, he would go down to where they sat behind the pulpit to talk. And his mother, as she saw from behind the lattice how he stood there exposed and small among his peers, most of whom were wrapped in the prayer shawls worn by married men, her heart wept within her.

The old man Shmuel-Meir, who was a longtime friend of the widow's family, for years would come over there after Sabbath had ended for a glass of tea.

In the past, when Yerucham-David was still alive, a pleasant sense of well-being would suffuse those evenings, along with that special mood in which the sacred and the profane mingle.

People were still dressed in their Sabbath finery, but steam from the simmering samovar was already rising over the table, and the host and his guest, over glasses of tea, played chess on the checkered board that was set into the middle of the table. Their combat was good-natured, without the storminess of war, punctuated by rabbinic proverbs or jokes, and in the meantime

Sarah-Leah, a strand of pearls around her throat, was preparing the post-Sabbath meal in the kitchen, or else she was arranging the Sabbath goblets in the glassed-in breakfront amidst a silvery tinkle that set the heart at ease.

Now there was gloom in the house.

Sarah-Leah's pearls were tucked away in the moneylender's strongbox, and the breakfront, without the glitter of the silver vessels, stood cold and shadowy, and only the luster of the friendship of the old man Shmuel-Meir had not dulled. And he, diligently stirring the watery tea he was served, just as if it had been sweetened, as before, with a generous hand, would ask Chaim-Raphael how his business was going and pass along some advice—he was a man of experience with a good sense for such things—and then, in order to raise their spirits, he would talk about what he had seen and heard in the course of the week. And they, out of respect for him, would listen attentively and even contribute a few words from time to time, although their minds, as could be seen from the expressions on their faces, often drifted far off from such matters.

And once, after such a tea party, during which the old man had heard more of the surging of their hearts than he did of their words, he went into the shop of Isser Levin, the man in whose house Fradl had been raised, and made the suggestion that to his mind seemed perfectly appropriate.

For the person in question, Chaim-Raphael, was a good sort, and the families on both sides have long and distinguished pedigrees—the match would be like a graft of two strong grapevines.

But the proud grocer answered with such an emphatic no that the old man recoiled, as if someone had thrown a stone at him, and walked out without saying good-bye, and he carried that humiliation in his heart for a long time.

It was different with Sarah-Leah, who showed no signs of anger when word of the story reached her, and who continued to speak with members of the Levin family with as good a temper as before, and she also treated Fradl warmly when she returned to live next door—although Fradl, actually, seemed somewhat estranged—and would bring her from time to time homemade pastries or preserves. And the neighbor women, who saw this, were amazed at her good nature, and some of them noted that although she was named after two of the biblical matriarchs, by her deeds she was equal to all four of them together.

In the third year of her marriage Fradl gave birth to a son, and the dark house, which had always seemed to be shadowed by a cloud, rang with joy.

Aunt Chana closed her millinery shop and arrived to tie on Fradl's apron, and very soon the smell of cinnamon and warm honey suffused the house.

On the line, in the yard, all the infant clothes that had been tucked away for a long time were hung for all to see, and in the evening the nighttime prayers of the little boys from the cheders rang out, and Mirl, the child of Chana's old age—she was as young as they were—passed out sweets with an embarrassed smile.

It was a great moment when the child, during the circumcision ceremony, was named for his mother's father, Barukh-Leyb, who was called "the Strongman" for the bravery of his heart, and who had passed away in his prime.

When the weakened Fradl's cries joined those of the infant, Avraham-Noach looked at her with eyes moist with pardon and trembling, and the rebbetzin, who was among the invited guests, said that now the break had been set right and the bond between the two of them would henceforth be solid.

Now came days that were like a holiday for those to whom an eldest son has been born.

The fancy tablecloth had not yet been removed from the table, and relatives and friends who stopped in were treated there to wine and pastries, amid preparations for the celebration, when the infant would be a month old, of the "redemption of the firstborn son."

The custom of the Levin family was to celebrate this ritual with a great banquet and invited guests, and so the large pots were taken down from the kitchen shelves, and from the nearest town the woman Toybe, a seasoned cook, was brought over —and then the child fell ill.

In the evening the sound of women cooking up a storm in the kitchen could still be heard and by the morning Avraham-Noach was already seen running to the doctor with galoshes on his bare feet, and then the sound of weeping echoed through the rooms and the house was plunged again into shadow.

When an infant dies before he reaches his first month, there are no elaborate mourning customs—and so the rooms were cleared of everything with which they had been filled. The servant girl took down to the poor people in the gulch all the appetizers and cakes, which now would not be needed, and Avraham-Noach began to go out in public again. He worked at his business and went to the community house for a little conversation, or else he would go down to the town garbage

dump, to Zanvil Elke's, who had recently returned from yeshiva and was always ready for a game of chess.

From a square of cardboard they cut out the pieces that
would represent the pawns, the knights, and bishops, and sent
forth these troops against each other with the cool poise of
seasoned military commanders, and sometimes they sat over
the board so far into the night that the footsteps of the butchers
rang out as they walked to the slaughterhouse after midnight,
at which point Elke, the mother, would wake up and start
grumbling about how they were wasting her kerosene and then
the guest would get up, unwillingly draw on his coat, and go.

"Mixed-up" Gitl, Fradl's neighbor on the kitchen side, once
saw him steal into the house through the back entrance, and
then from inside came the sound of words and a moaning cry,
and the next day she told the women about it at the community
bench, where the relations between the couple was by now a
frequent subject, and little Chana, who was playing there, listened to the story.

In that place, in those days, they did not believe in shielding
the eyes of a child by throwing an elegant prayer shawl over
life's nakedness, and so, along with the song of sun-dazzled
birds and the scent of dew-drunk plants, she also absorbed impressions of daily life, bits of local color, of heartache and heart
joy, which in the course of time—when they had been refined
and illuminated by the light of her intellect, and experience had
bound them into life stories—became for her, in the solitary
nights of her wandering, a source of pleasure and comfort.

In those days Fradl was no longer as beautiful as she had once
been, the light in her shining light-blue eyes had been dimmed,

and her body, like a plant that has not been watered for many days, had gone slack and lost its flexibility, and one could see from her knitting, as she sat on the bench outside, that she kept it up only for the sake of appearances, for the stitches did not match up and the spool of yarn grew no smaller.

In the afternoon hours Aunt Racha would sometimes come by, the wife of Isser Levin—a woman as intelligent and tough as he was. And then the two of them would go into a small side room, and they would stay there for a long time, and Fradl, when she came out to see her visitor to the front gate, her face looked as if it had been washed after a cry.

Once Avraham-Noach's sister came to visit for a few days from the district capital.

She was elegantly tall with uncovered blond hair she wore in thick curls—at her side her brother's face glowed, as if it were reflecting her radiance.

On the Sabbath the two of them sang the Sabbath hymns together, as they had in their parents' house, he in a deep bass and she in the tones of a harp.

For the first time since the man had come to live in that house, the sound of singing emerged from there, and the neighbors, in the course of their Sabbath strolls, drew near and saw, standing at the front door, Fradl, still and cold in a dark kerchief that cast a pall across her face—a shadow.

Aunt Chana, who knew the visitor a little, as she often traveled to the provincial capital on store business, came by the next day, since she had heard that the woman was getting ready to leave. And when she saw Fradl lying down, flattened with melancholy, a bandage tied to her aching forehead, she drew the city woman into the next room and asked her, speaking laconically because of the constraints of time, if she had done something to help her, for surely she could see what was becoming of the woman.

But she, fixing her with her intelligent eyes, responded with another question:

"What could she do? When things had come to such a pass," she said, "could anyone ever really take responsibility for another person in affairs of the heart?"

And after a slight hesitation she added with a sigh, very seriously, that in her opinion it would be better if they were to separate. "Neither he nor she had any other real alternative," she pronounced, and with that she walked out and went her way, for her carriage had arrived.

After that it became perfectly clear to the members of the family that there was no hope left for the woman, and Aunt Racha, her confidante, made no attempt to shield Fradl from that fact. But she, like a sick person whom the doctors had given up on, tried a number of other various remedies: She had a few dresses made up, as people did then, in fiery colors, although they only accentuated her pallor, and she, when she was told that a man likes a woman with some meat on her bones—began to fill herself up with fattening cereals and thick cream soups.

On the step, at the entrance to the kitchen, was where she usually sat, swallowing slowly from the full bowl with such a grimace of distaste that whoever saw her would be unable to touch that particular food again.

It was especially difficult to see her obsequiously hurry to bring him, her husband, his coat or umbrella because it had begun to rain—which he waved away in protest, by the way—

or when she squeezed herself to the side to make room for him when she saw him coming as she sat on the step.

The post or the door against which she was leaning would then become a depression into which she pressed to make herself yet a little smaller and more insubstantial, and at those moments, as those who watched shook their heads, there remained no compassion, only scorn, the emotion aroused in everyone by the despised one in the Bible, like Leah who degrades and humiliates herself by chasing after a little husbandly affection.

Those whose hearts were no longer touched by the fate of the woman watched her struggles only out of curiosity, the way one might follow a character in a novel. And there were some among them who really found in it the stimulation and spicy plot of a romance. For after all, did they not also have before their eyes the figure of Chaim-Raphael the neighbor, with his "deafness" toward everything that touched upon the matter of marriage. He, whose afflicted face made him seem like a person for whom life was an uncharted wilderness.

With what careless abandon he stood on the dilapidated bridge, at the very height of the breakup of the river ice, and how eagerly he pursued every opportunity, as a member of "Hospice for the Poor," to care for precisely those sick people afflicted with the most contagious conditions.

During a fire, he was seen jumping into a burning building in order to save a few petty household items, and his mother, Sarah-Leah, when she saw that he was taking his time inside, climbed up herself onto the ladder that led to the opening.

She stood afterward on the nearby grassy field and wrung out the places on his clothes that were still smoking, and then the old man Shmuel-Meir approached them and rebuked him, the young man, angrily, which was not his usual way.

"Have you forgotten the commandment 'And you shall guard your own souls'?" he said.

And he, his mouth twisting, looked at him and laughed a strange laugh, like Crazy Chaim-Zelig during a heat wave.

Once, it was in the summertime, Avraham-Noach suddenly fell ill in the middle of the night.

It seemed to him as he slept that someone was stabbing him in the side with a knife, and when he awoke he felt as if that entire part of his body were about to split open, and he was seized by a choking sensation, and deathly terror.

Fradl, who had also awakened, got out of bed and stood over him in alarm, and so as not to be oppressed with her questions, he tried to restrain himself and swallow the pain, but when it grew stronger he asked for a doctor to be called, and she—the maid was sleeping in her own house at the out-skirts of the shtetl that night—went outside and looked in both directions, mentally weighing which way to turn. But since the nearby houses all stood closed and shuttered, as if estranged from her, she turned and climbed the porch steps of the factory owner's house, and as she had before in the time of the catas-trophe, when her mother and father had left her, she knocked softly on the glass door there. And the man there, inside—as if he had been awake and waiting for the knock—immediately dressed, took up his stick to defend himself against the dogs of unfamiliar streets, and went to get the doctor, and also went to the pharmacy to buy the medicines, and then he sat by himself in the big room and waited, in case he should be needed for something else.

The servant girl, when she came in at daybreak, was amazed to see the strange neighbor sitting, absolutely still, eyes closed as if he were dreaming, and she walked over and extinguished the lamp that was burning at one side of the room, at which point the man turned gray, awoke, arose, and walked out.

And Fradl, as her husband rallied, and he could take something to eat from her hand, her spirits were revived.

She herself swept and scrubbed his room, and drew aside or raised or lowered the curtain on the window as he wished, walking about in light house-slippers to keep down the noise, looking as if she were floating on air.

From the attic she took down the folding chair, in which one could both recline and lie down, and as soon as the patient could get up and stand on his legs she took this reclining chair out to the side of the yard where the climbing vines from the widow's garden cast their shade, and she also brought out one of the little ottomans, so that the man could eat his meals on it as on a table.

But as soon as the man got a whiff of fresh air, he stood up and crossed the synagogue square at a diagonal and, to the astonishment of the people watching him, walked down toward Zanvil Elke's room at the edge of the garbage dump.

He was still unsteady on his feet, but his chess partner, who came out to greet him, supported him as the two of them walked over to the shack where the wild dogs emerged to circle him, and a dust cloud from the community garbage whirled around him in the breeze.

Now the servant girl could put the dishes back in their places and walk around the rooms in her nailed shoes without fear of disturbing anyone's rest.

At that time Aunt Chana was about to leave for the village of Kaminka for an engagement party at the house of one of her relatives, and Fradl went to help her with the preparations for travel, and in the course of that day she was not seen in the alley, until the neighbors were sure that she too had gone off with her aunt. But later that evening, when Mixed-up Gitl approached the shared fence, she saw a kind of housedress lying there on the other side, and thinking that a piece of laundry had been left there, she stooped and was about to pick it up, and then the dress moved, and what revealed itself from within it convulsed before her like someone in the spasms of death. Then the God-struck woman clapped her hands together and ran quickly to the community house, where a few Talmud students were passing a friendly hour, and called out in a horrified voice:

"Come and look how he butchered her now."

And she gestured toward Avraham-Noach, who was among the group seated there.

And the rebbetzin, who understood that the woman had been "visited by the spirit," called to her in soothing tones:

"Gitl, Gitl."

And she drew her behind the partition of the women's section and soothed her until she calmed down.

But the people there, around the table, could not find the thread of their conversation again and so, one by one, they got up and left, as if in shame.

At about that time Mordechai Katz bought the tar furnaces in the Kochticzy Forest from the Zarczya farm, and invited Avraham-Noach to be his manager and bookkeeper. And he accepted.

A house had not yet been set up for a family, and so the man prepared to go out there on his own for the present, and he packed up everything he thought he would need, and Fradl stood by his side and helped him.

It was something of a shoal this, amidst the angry waves surrounding them, and they, exhausted from their struggles, both took their rest on it.

For in his mind's eye he already saw himself in the refuge of the abundant fields of Zarczya and felt the contact of men with whom he shared a bond of affection.

Fradl passed the pressing iron over his linens and in a special basket prepared all sorts of pastries as snacks for him, and on the day of his departure she accompanied him to the hotel at the edge of the town, where the farm's carriage awaited him. And this time the two of them walked together, abreast, not as on their holiday visits, when he would race ahead of her or dawdle, following far behind.

While the driver was dealing with the horses in the yard of the hotel, he loaded his suitcases in and prepared himself a place to sit, and when the carriage finally departed toward the high road he turned toward the place where she stood and waved his fine handkerchief at her, and this noble gesture was engraved within her as a token of goodwill, a sort of waving of the white flag to signal a bid for peace.

As one among the many women whose husbands were off somewhere, in distant regions, she began to live, from this point, a "paper life": she waited for the postman or for the carriage drivers who passed by the Kochticzy Forest, where the tar furnaces were.

The letters she received were short, but she valued them, and she read their lines and between the lines, in an attempt to find something there which could resonate with the feelings in her own heart.

In the autumn he moved to the new place and he promised to come home for Passover, but the road happened to be blocked due to a flooded river and the visit was postponed to the Shavuot holiday. And then the man who was supposed to take over for him fell ill and now again he was unable to set a date for his arrival.

In any case the house was neat and always stood ready. The pantry was full of all sorts of food that could keep and the furniture was draped with holiday covers, and to keep the other rooms tidy she ate her meals in the kitchen, at the edge of the table—a provisional eating, as on the eve of a holiday, when the important meal is reserved for later on, for the anticipated celebratory hour.

At the same time she dressed in her good clothing and was found more and more at the market—in Isser Levin's store or at her aunt Chana's, places that had a good view of the high road and where one could see every passing carriage.

And one day the carriage of the Zarczya farm indeed appeared, with the man and his traveling case inside.

Leybl, the child of Isser Levin's old age, was the one who noticed it first, and he ran ahead of the horses to pass along the news, and there, in the house, Fradl was already appearing at the front door, her brushed silk headkerchief glistening on her head like a halo.

The master's carriage was brought into the yard, and the practical and efficient Aunt Chana could be seen making her way among the curious and turning toward the community house.

For the woman, who had not purified herself according to Jewish law before her husband's arrival, was forbidden to him, and so the aunt had been sent by her to the rabbi on some matter regarding her ritual immersion, and the response came that she would be permitted to immerse. And then, after the visitor had eaten a little something and rested and gone off to take care of his business, she went out, a small package in hand, to the end of the alley, where the bathhouse stood open, one of its sections heated.

About this commandment, and how the daughters of Israel in the shtetls fulfilled it, it's worth writing a special section.

They, these shy women, who concealed themselves within their kitchens, would make their way, when the time came, through the alleyways to the bathhouse before the eyes of the curious, each of whom knew them by name.

The kerchief was too small to obscure their flushed, shamed faces, and the ground beneath was stiff and unforgiving and so slippery that it was easy to trip.

And behind them, had they not left a house in disorder, a goat waiting to be milked, hungry children crying for their supper, and an unperturbed husband who paid them no mind? He was a moody man, who did not pamper his household or speak softly to them, and against him the heart swelled with rage. And indeed it was not the desire for a little lovemaking that propelled these women, but rather the holy duty, the inheritance of their mothers, the commandment of life itself.

And these were the women who raised clear-eyed sons, weaned them, and fed them on suffering. The sons were washed not with water but in their mother's tears, and they were sated, in the absence of bread, on the sorrow of her love, which they absorbed like nectar of the gods.

There were some among these sons who were overtaken and slaughtered by violent gentiles, but there were also some among them who went out at such times with an outstretched hand and were a shield and savior to their brothers, or else, with the redeemers of their homeland, prepared themselves to work the soil and provide a place to settle for the rest of their nation, who were perched, wherever they were, at the edge of an abyss.

And so Fradl, after she too had taken the tortuous road described above, and then come out again after her immersion, fingernails clipped and her hair dripping wet—and there was still some light left in the day—she turned to walk along the winding path through the gardens, whose owners had already gone inside by this hour.

And meanwhile at the house, the maid had wisely provided bread and meat for the carriage driver and water for the horses and set the table neatly and tastefully, as she assumed her mistress would have done—and then the man came in from the street in a flurry and asked that he be given his suitcases, because he was going to have to leave. And he had already ordered the driver to harness the horse and also gone out himself, wrapped in his overcoat, and Fradl appeared at that instant as she arrived home. Then he told her he had something to take care of in the village of Kaminka, and that there were businessmen waiting for him there, and shortly after that the carriage left with a hurried trot through the alley.

Through the clouds of dust the faces of the dumbstruck people peered as if through a fog, and an anticipatory stillness settled there, as after a murderous blow had fallen on someone, while those who stood around listened for the groan in reaction, which is the sign of life.

Mixed-up Gitl, who was standing beside the shared fence, called out in her piercing voice:

"You see, I told you he was a murderer, and now he's really spilled her blood."

And she pointed toward the window where the red of the sunset was reflected, and then the maid appeared and pulled at the cords and the curtain fell.

And Aunt Chana, who had been called by one of the neighbors, came and could be heard there, inside, her words falling on deaf ears, for the woman, as later was told, just paced back and forth in her room groaning little truncated groans, from between clenched lips, like someone trying to overcome their pain, and every time the aunt tried to come near her she gently pushed her aside, politely, until the woman, exhausted with grief and the day's exertions, finally went over to one of the couches, reclined at one end of it, and fell asleep. When she later awoke, in the morning light, something happened that at first frightened her, as she told it, because she found her niece sitting at the table that was still laid out from the day before, hungrily eating everything that had been prepared there. But after she noticed her bright face and the clarity of her mind the woman understood that something had taken shape within her niece in the course of that night, the thing that her enlightened daughters later called a turning point, but which in her opinion was nothing more than the little common sense the Lord had put in her heart.

The members of Isser Levin's household were surprised then to see Fradl come in, wearing, unusually enough, a simple dress, one she had saved from her girlhood days, and she, going off into a side room with her aunt and confidante, spent a long time in there with her. And when they finally emerged the two of them announced together, cheerfully, that it was time to go about arranging a divorce. And Uncle Isser was commissioned to act as intermediary in the negotiations with "the other party."

While her uncle was involved with handling the divorce, Fradl slowly but surely "purified" the house. She cleared out everything that had been purchased for his comfort, sold the dresses in which she had gussied herself up to attract him or gave them away to poor women, and then took his letters out of the desk drawers, those he had sent during their engagement and those he had written afterward, and sent them all up in flames. She piled up the kindling and twigs so the flames would reach high, and she stood and watched his deceit, his empty tokens of love, and his broken promises go up in smoke. And her face, with her pale blue eyes, shone at that moment like the face of her father when he, in his time, went out to avenge himself against the gentiles up the mountain who oppressed him continually through no fault of his own.

And then the day came when she stood in the community house, before the eyes of all who had assembled for the ceremony, and received her divorce. She was dressed simply, as in her girlhood, and now that she had regained her recognition of her own worth, she stood straight and tall once again. And people said that she was more beautiful than on her wedding day.

After all this the events came to pass that many had long anticipated:

Isser Levin went into old Shmuel-Meir's house and settled the matter that he had suggested to him years before.

And with that the fence that separated the lots of Fradl and the widow was taken down, and the two large houses at the center of the alley became as one.

Sarah-Leah, whose face regained the radiance it had once held in good times past, now lavished treats on Fradl even more tenderly than she had in her childhood, and she was the one who raised for her Yerucham-David, her son, a beautiful child who even when he was very young showed signs of the strength of his maternal grandfather, and when some fight broke out between the gentile urchins and the little cheder boys, he was always at their head. And Chana, who in the meantime had gone off to distant regions, was told that he was the one, when he grew up, who taught the young men of the town the tactics of self-defense.

For in those days the surrounding gentiles sought pretexts against the townspeople and their thirst for Jewish blood grew.

And when they gathered and came here with their weapons of destruction, those brave boys went out to meet them, with Yerucham-David, Fradl's son, at their head, and they chased them away and the town was quiet.

Bill of Divorcement

Of all the people who came before my father's rabbinic court, the women who were about to be sent away from their husbands' homes seemed to me the most afflicted.

Certainly there were others who had been robbed of justice: workers whose bosses had exploited them or peddlers who had been cheated, but those people stood some chance of seeing their situations rectified.

The arguments were laid out and the witnesses testified and the ones found culpable were obliged to pay. The law was on the side of those who had been wronged.

But for these women, refugees of the heart, as they were called, the judgment was harsh.

"If a man takes a wife," it is written, "and she fails to please him, he writes for her a bill of divorcement."

And really, what remedy can there be for the absence of love?

It is a terminal illness and whomever it afflicts will never recover again.

For five or ten years the woman kept her home and watched over the man's peace and comfort. She laundered, she darned, she patched. With industrious hands she ironed out the complicated and smoothed down the rough.

She gathered a few sticks for fuel at building sites, she collected kitchen scraps from backyards as compost for her vegetable bed, where she grew beans, carrots, and radishes, and from these poor ingredients she whipped up a vegetable soup or a fruit compote. From nothing, she created something.

And when the man came in, sat down at the table she had set, cut himself a slice of bread with his strong hands, and gulped down the soup she served him, and through the steam rising from the bowl he would cast a glance in her direction in which a hint of contentment or gratitude flickered—this would be her reward.

But it sometimes happened that, one day, all of it fell apart. Whether under the influence of members of his family, who harbored hateful thoughts toward the woman, or because he had found "another, more suitable woman"—his feelings were turned on their head. And without that special ingredient that can turn the bitter sweet, everything became flat and tasteless.

The bread was suddenly deemed scorched, or half-baked, and the main dish was overcooked and smelled off—and the argument broke out. At first it was hushed, because they were embarrassed in front of the neighbors, and then later, when the bitterness had accumulated in their hearts—it raged and thundered like those heavy clouds that, when lightning strikes, disintegrate into a frenzied storm.

If there were children there, they huddled like chicks in a downpour that threatens their nest. They were overcome with pity for their mother, terror at their father's wrath.

That man, in the madness of his rage, knowing that this was a way to wound her, sometimes lashed out at them too, beating them mercilessly.

One of the neighbors would intervene and bring them into their house, where they would sit unclaimed the whole day through like objects abandoned by their owner until night fell, and only then would they gather up their nerve to go home. They felt their way in the darkness to their beds and crept under the covers in mute terror, and then the mother would sit up where she was and understand that things couldn't go on this way, someone would have to put a stop to it. And soon the day would come when she stepped out her door and made her way toward the community house.

How did she feel, walking this road of sorrow, at whose end lay her expulsion from her house?

The grocer at the corner of the community-house alley went out to stand at his door to sneak a look at her, and from the bakery stoop, further down the alley, the woman, his wife, came down to greet her.

They had never been very close friends, but now she came and scrutinized her with that look that, to a stricken person, feels like fingers probing a wound.

The beadle in the yard of the rabbinic courthouse, a familiar face, was now pretending not to know her. He was in his official role now, and the building itself, when she entered it, felt like a bridge with no railings for support, a dizzying walk over the terrifying abyss.

The scribe's implements on the table; the sharp, opened pen-knife glinting among them; the judge's bench, just as she had always imagined the Heavenly Court before which she was destined to stand when her time came; and the icy chill that came from the corner where he sat, fortified by the members of his family, who formed a wall around him now.

Those people—if there was any enmity between them and the woman, they could not hide their satisfaction now. The man was a link that had been ripped from its chain, and now he was back where he belonged, linked up with them again.

They had already slipped a bottle of water into his pocket early that morning, so that he could wash his hands the minute he had handed over the divorce decree and thus "be the first to grab the good luck," and then one of them disappeared to bring liquor and cake, stepping behind the wooden partition to our part of the house to ask for glasses and a tray.

My mother, who was ordinarily so gracious and even-tempered, would simply refuse.

"That cupboard is just too hard to reach," she would reply. And instead, as the preparations for drawing up the divorce decree came to an end, she would bring the woman into her own part of the house.

The meadow opened out here beyond the window, and over the sofa where she had seated the woman she could see it, in the summer, with its lush grass, stretching out into the ample expanses with an innocent serenity, not identifying in the least with the twisted paths of the human heart or its troubles:

The water-filled ditches that lay so calmly there, bordering the gardens, with the reflected radiance of the sky flickering within them, and the solitary linden tree beside them, the sight of which might arouse encouraging thoughts, since undoubtedly the stormy gales had unleashed their fury upon it more than once, and nevertheless there it was, still standing.

Mother, seeing the thoughtful expression the woman was wearing, disappeared from the room.

The place where a person communes with their heart is holy—she believed—and no stranger should approach it.

But now the silence had finally ended there, on the other side of the partition, and the final hour had come, heavy with fate and the full severity of the law.

The Hebrew words were read aloud, the witnesses arose to affix their signatures, and the man, standing with a quorum of men around him, handed his wife the bill of divorcement, explicitly pronouncing her divorced and cast off from him, and now the circle opened around her and she was pushed out of it and stood isolated, and she stumbled about a little this way and that before she found her way out the door.

My mother—if it was already after nightfall—set the lantern out on the windowsill, but the ray it cast across the path outside was empty. She dropped out of sight and was swallowed by the darkness.

And then there would be a sequel. A few women, either because they felt sorry for her or because their own marriages were less than entirely happy, decided to do something to improve her situation. They supplied her with some dry goods or foodstuffs and she set out to peddle this merchandise, but there was nothing that could really set things right again.

Her hands grew tired from holding up a home that had lost its central pillar, and everything began to seem vacuous:

The dining table on Sabbaths and holidays, the bedside of a sick child and the bench outside, where they had taken the breeze on summer evenings.

And then, of course, there were the dreams, recurring images, echoes of what had once been:

A warm gaze through the window as she came back in the morning from market. Bathing a child together, shoulder to shoulder in the hot steam rising from the basin, and his loyal shudder at the sound of the stifled cry of her pain.

With the fragments of such reflections still within her she stood the next morning by her basket and haggled with customers, her eye caught by every thread of smoke rising from his chimney, every half-shadow in which she'd see his figure.

And sometimes, in some nearby alley, bending over to look at their child, she would see him and, for a moment, they'd be united by a common love.

"So not everything has been cut off," she would stop short, excited. "So why, then? Why has it come to this?"

But it also sometimes happened that, among the people coming and going in the streets, she would see a small child one day with a face just like his, and he—looked just like the son who was walking with her, at her side, and then the child would be told:

"Look, it's your brother. Go give him a nice kiss," and the earth would crumble beneath her feet.

There was yet another kind of woman who was sentenced to divorce: the women who had been with their husbands for ten years without having children. For these women, the amputation scar never healed.

Among these women I remember the peddler Zlateh who lived in the gulch—a brave soul who was always in good spirits.

At one time she had married someone from the neighborhood, Isser Ber was his name, an unemployed bookbinder.

For years she had pursued him—they said—and finally she had won her heart's desire, and after that she was fueled by the same spirit with which the biblical Jacob rolled the heavy boulder from the mouth of the well.

She easily hoisted her two baskets, filled to the brim with fruits and vegetables.

Between buying and selling, she washed strangers' laundry by the riverbank, and at night she kneaded rye dough at the baker's, earning, in addition to a few copper coins, a small loaf baked from the remnants of the dough, and this she ate afterward with her Isser Ber (in the summer, under the pear tree outside), passing him slice after slice, and the scent of love arose from there, mingling with the smell of the meal she had cooked overnight in the baker's oven.

The people who lived in the neighborhood, as they came and went, would rest their gaze on them with the same radiant faces with which they would look at a blossoming tree or at a garden drunk with sunlight and dew.

But here, in the meantime, the years were passing, and the still childless woman had no idea that their limit had already been set and was rapidly approaching.

Her body was worn out and she was also a few years older than the man, and the other members of his family looked and saw now that the family tree—one of its limbs was in danger of withering.

When the tenth year came, the designated one, his relatives

came from the village of Kaminka and took him home with them, and she, in her naïveté, was happy about that.

"Let him get a little fresh air," she said.

And she would send him challahs every Sabbath with a braid of dough on top, the kind he liked, and also—to stimulate his appetite—some herring, which was hard to come by over there in the village.

On the day he was supposed to come home she happened to find, in the market, a few cherries from the Countess's garden, and her eyes shone as brightly as the dewy fruit she was carrying home.

I'll boil them for my Isser Ber, she thought; he loves cherry jam.

And as she was boiling them later, standing over the stove with her cheeks flushed, she was surprised to see her two brothers-in-law from Kaminka enter, their faces as hard as someone about to execute a sentence, with Isser Ber himself walking behind them, his eyes averted and his face quivering like a flame exposed to a blast of chilly air.

I saw the woman on the morning of her divorce, as she stood waiting to come into the courtroom inside our house.

The scribe, at the community table, was just beginning to sharpen his knife at that moment, and she lurched like a bull being led into the slaughterhouse, when he gets his first whiff of warm blood.

"No, no," she said.

And my mother, who was standing in the doorway of the room, took a step backward and quickly turned her face aside.

A young girl had already been arranged for the man, a girl

whose sisters were fertile women who had borne many sons, and he was quickly brought to the wedding canopy with her. And before the year was out, she was sitting on the bench beside their house—she was the daughter of Jonah the carpenter, from our alley—a sturdy baby boy on her lap.

People remembered for a long time afterward the commotion in the synagogue the Sabbath she came to services for the first time after the birth.

She was wearing a new dress she had sewn herself, which all the women took notice of, since she was a seamstress who knew what sorts of things they were wearing in the city, and suddenly from the corner where the peddler woman was sitting a strange cough could be heard, and then the sobs broke out—the kind of wailing that wells up from the depths and repels all attempts at consolation and subduing and makes everyone who hears it doubt that the world is truly as it should be.

They tried to go over to the woman afterward and soothe her. She was offered a prime spot in the market, and then the baker from her neighborhood wanted to hire her as his regular housekeeper, but when she did not respond—they left her alone, the way people let a house in flames burn itself out once it no longer poses a threat to others—and she continued to flicker until she was finally extinguished.

It happened on a summer morning, the rasp of the saw and sander and a trill of song broke forth from the carpentry shop, and now along came someone from the gulch and went into the workshop and the ruckus stopped, and after that the funeral procession passed through the alley, a loner's funeral, with no eulogy and no tears.

The people, those who were busy working, came and stood

in their doorways while others came out and walked with the procession until the crossroad, and after that a silence fell, in which, like static in a telegraph line, thoughts hummed and throbbed.

The peddler woman's neighbor, Esther the bagel seller, finally put the essence of these thoughts into words, turning either to the carpentry shop or to the community house to ask why they hadn't just killed that woman right then and there? Why the agony of a long, slow death?

"If you cut off someone's head," she said angrily, the tears flowing, "then do it, at least, with one stroke."

Family

Concerning the chain of generations, how it takes shape and grows, the Bible only tells us briefly that a certain man lived for so many years and he begot a son, and then this son lived for so many years and he begot sons and daughters.

Link after link in a chain that never stops, for even if it breaks, it always renews itself. Such a genealogy looks something like this:

To Adam were born Cain and Abel and Seth; and Cain begot Enoch, the same Enoch in whose lifetime his father built a city. And Seth begot Enosh, and Enosh begot Kenan, and Kenan begot Mahalalel, and Mahalalel begot Jared, and Jared lived 162 years and he begot—Enoch . . .

Another little Enoch, who probably ran about barefoot all day on the warm grass, and in the evening fell asleep on his loving mother's lap, just like that other Enoch, in whose lifetime the city was built.

In my shtetl, where people were named after their late fore-fathers, this pattern was even clearer.

There was the baker, for instance, from whom I bought my rye bread every day: he was known as Leyzer son of Chaim son of Meir.

Leyzer, who was sixty, only brought the water from the well for kneading the dough; it was his oldest son, Meir, who baked and sold the bread, and he also had a young son who was still learning at the cheder—Chaim.

The family had been bakers for generations; the order of things only changed in that when one of the Meirs grew weak and full of years, he would go out to draw the water and his son, Chaim, would bake the bread, and when Chaim grew old, he would fetch the water, and his son, Leyzer, would bake the bread.

In my childhood it was Leyzer who brought the water from the well. He was a gray-haired man who walked slowly, his stooped back a perfect fit for the curve of the yoke.

Years later, when I returned from traveling in distant regions, it was Meir I found walking slowly with a stooped back. Leyzer rested among his ancestors. To the row of graves in the cemetery had been added a stone carved with a pair of hands raised in the priestly benediction, for they were a family of priestly descent. His grandson, Chaim, did the baking now, and his wife was a powerful woman who carried the sacks of flour on her back even while she was pregnant, and everyone who saw her was stirred, for they knew: a little Leyzer was about to be born.

These were the generations of the family in the shtetl.

But sometimes it happened that there was no one to continue a family line, if God had denied them his blessing, and then it was as if a link had been dislocated and the whole chain was shaken.

In our alley, that was how it was with Barukh son of Avner son of Zevil.

Zevil, the grandfather, had built himself a house here, and when he died, he bequeathed it to his son Avner, since he was the firstborn and, moreover, he had the finest character and was the most respected of the brothers. They were all towering men, with thick beards that descended importantly onto their chests, and they were known as the "Beardites," or the "Levites," since their family belonged to the tribe of Levi, and they were such a large family that when they went up to wash the priests' hands in the synagogue before the priests blessed the congregation—it was so crowded around the bucket that each of them could only touch it with a single finger.

On Sabbaths and holidays they wore silk caftans and their wives wore stiff satin; the wives were large women, with sullen eyelids, but they had a kind gaze, and when they laughed, it was genuine.

Because they were so tall, they built themselves large houses, each house surrounded by a fenced-in yard with a woodshed and another shed for storing flax, since some of them were in the flax business, and on weekdays they would make the rounds of the villages while the women would be the ones to raise the children, and cook, bake, and go down to the riverbank to wash the clothes, and in the summer, they would also go out to work in their gardens, just a few beds where they grew radishes and onions, some vines and beanpoles, and also pumpkins, whose seeds were a treat to crack on Friday nights.

On Sundays, when they couldn't go around to the villages, the men worked on their accounts at home, sorted and counted the bundles of flax, chopped and stacked the week's firewood, and in the summer they even managed to get in a stroll down the street, wearing their Sabbath caftans over their work clothes, their faces still scrubbed from their Friday afternoon baths—and then it seemed as if they were adding a little of the week to the holy day.

Avner son of Zevil indeed cut the most imposing figure of the brothers, and people felt safe walking at his side. He emanated power and conviction, and he carried an oak walking stick, six feet long, the way another man might carry a weapon. Once, during a riot, he used it to beat the liquor out of a few hoodlums from up the hill, until they were ready to kiss the hem of his caftan, and after that, whenever they saw him on the street, they left a wide berth around him, smiling strangely as they passed.

"And Jethro trembled," declared the learned old Shloyme, Avner's scholarly uncle, who could find an appropriate biblical verse for every occasion.

Avner died when he was still in his prime of the common cold, after stumbling, on a rainy day, into a marsh in the forest. The Polish medic from the mountain applied cupping glasses and gave him concoctions to raise a sweat, and Avner drank and sweated, but even so he saw himself still wandering, lost, through the marshes, without a path, dark waves encircling him.

"I am sinking into the slimy deep," he remembered the words from Psalms, and he strove to reach the middle of the chapter: "Let the floodwaters not sweep me away," and then the fluids rose in his throat and he awoke, spitting blood.

He was a widower, and his two married daughters, Musha and Mechla, who had hurried over from their husbands' houses, secluded themselves in the storage shed, where they could sit and weep:

"Oh, father mine."

Then they put their minds to helping him recover and cooked him some chicken soup, each in her own home, and he drank a little of each soup and asked them to call his uncle Shloyme, the oldest member of the family, so that he could settle his affairs.

"Do not let the thread be broken," he said, gesturing like someone snapping a thread. "Take a wife for my son Barukh."

And on that very same day, Musha, the older daughter, tied a shawl over her best satin dress and went over to a nearby town, where a match had been proposed for her brother, and what a relief it was when the matter was settled. Old Shloyme, who had also been sent for, was immediately smitten with the bride-to-be's father, a man weak in body but with a strong mind, able to answer any halakhic question trenchantly and with ease.

He was a poor schoolteacher of the youngest children and he had no dowry to offer, but he was persuaded to pay for a satin wedding dress, which was tastefully made, with a lace sash and a delicate ruffle at the collar.

The wedding was celebrated on the first day of Elul, and the bride was brought to her father-in-law's house—a tender young thing who was still unaccustomed to the burden of hair covering, and she would lift her hands every few moments to adjust her kerchief with heartbreaking shyness. She had been raised by a stepmother, and her face, with its dark shadows under the eyes, was the face of an unloved baby; on weekdays, the tall women of her in-laws' family would go over to greet her, wiping their hands on their aprons, and their kind, hearty laughter would chase away the shadows that hung over her.

On the eve of Yom Kippur, the dying man was still able to gather enough strength to stand up and bless her. He spread his veined hands, which were as gnarled and dry as the bark on a withered tree, and stood over her, like a tree that was shedding its leaves:

"May God make you as Sarah and Rebecca," he said, "like Rachel and Leah," and wave after icy wave flooded over her, and she was filled with a chilly dread all that day.

After the High Holidays the man died and was gathered unto his fathers, to the row of Levites in the cemetery, whose tombstones bore the names, in alternating order, as in life: Zevil, Barukh, Shloyme. A little distance away, off to one side, stood the grave markers of infants who had died before their time, and the tall women wailed over them and beat their breasts, which sounded like a flurry of wings among the trees. Winter was already approaching, and lifeless leaves drifted onto the mourners from above, light as feathers.

When the thirty days of mourning were over, the house and everything in it were thoroughly washed, and the young wife— Dinah was her name—began to unpack her belongings.

She had indeed been given no dowry, but she owned a few

of the things she had made in the evenings at her girlfriends' houses: lace tablecloths and runners for the table and sideboard, pillowcases with patchwork appliqué, and a wall hanging with an embroidered proverb to adorn the wall.

On the windowsills she placed a few houseplants, and in the bedroom she hung a thick pleated partition. It was not a spacious room, but it was nicely arranged, with a three-legged table in one corner and a colorful rug between the two beds.

On Friday afternoons she could now wash her hair in private, undisturbed. She would pull the shade over the window, and in the dim half-light, she would let down her copious hair and stand for a while before the mirror, which was also full of shadowy light, like that shimmering light at sunset. Fine steam rose from the basin, and, right there, beside it, on its colored paper, the "good" soap lay exposed, its embossed surface still showing.

Barukh, peering into her corner, felt something like what he had once experienced when he had walked into the pine forest just as the sun was rising. He was still young and didn't know how to speak about love, but now he truly understood what the Torah portion of the week meant when it told of Isaac, who brought Rebecca into the tent of his mother, Sarah, and he loved her and was comforted after his mother's death.

Since he had to recite the kaddish in the synagogue every day, he couldn't travel to the distant villages, and so it was arranged that he would only do business with the nearby farms, so he could go there and come back between the morning and afternoon prayers.

In the summer when the days grew longer, he could manage this without any trouble. After the sunrise service, he would

take the sack of flax and turn up the hillside road that took
him down to the villages. Dinah gave him a buckwheat cake,
or rye bread with cheese for the road, and as the sun began to
set, when it was time for the afternoon prayer, she would go
wait for him on the bench outside. The first of the congregants
would pass her on their way to synagogue. The Beardites, her
relatives, would nod to her gravely; and she would respond with
trepidation, feeling like an orphan; but now here was Barukh
coming toward her, dusty and strong, and she would reach up
to arrange her kerchief, and her mournful expression would
evaporate.

The sounds of prayer were sweet in the gathering dusk; they
surged from the schoolhouses like water roaring over a dam.
And soon enough the children came bursting out to spread
through the alley in clusters by age and grade: the boys in the
Bible class, the boys in the Hebrew class, and the boys in the
beginning Aleph Bet class. There were dozens, scores, legions
of them. "Fill the earth" had been God's first blessing—and
the strip of earth in the alley became full. Like the young shoots
of the fields they sprouted, like seedlings in a flower bed, and
when the occasional summer shower would fall, these boys
would be standing around the alley with their hands held out
in prayer:

"Oh God, send us your rain for the sake of your little children," and then it was clear that the rain had indeed come for
them.

Sometimes on a day like that a rainbow might appear on
high and stretch across the sky, clasping the town from one end
to the other in a powerful hoop. The thatched houses seemed
to shrink, and a strange luster illuminated the windowpanes.

Women, the light of grace on their faces, recited at the doors to their houses, "Blessed is He who remembers His covenant with Noah," while above them, the miraculous sign would deepen in color and intimate: "Never again will I curse the ground, so long as the earth endures, seedtime and harvest, cold and heat, summer and winter, day and night shall not cease."

When the afternoon prayer was over, Dinah would go inside to cook supper, a stew of barley and potatoes the locals called "krupnik." The children ate it sitting on their doorsteps, outside, from their unbreakable metal bowls. Here and there a small child would fall asleep while eating, and the mother would come and lift it up carefully, like a sack filled with a treasure, and carry it off to bed.

Barukh and Dinah would sit on their threshold until the alley emptied out. If there was a moon rising, it was as lonely in the sky as they were on the doorstep.

When the year of mourning was over, Barukh began to go out to the distant villages and one of the twin orphan girls that old Shloyme was raising in his house was sent to spend the night with Dinah.

Because of the evening chill, she would arrive in an oversized down jacket and a shawl but when she took all that off, you could see she was one of the family—she had heavy eyelids and a thick braid, and her laughter splashed and tinkled, making you think of a bubbling spring. Liebka was her name, an orphan girl who had never known a mother's love, and she would lean against Dinah gently, kiss the nape of her neck between her collar and kerchief, and call her "Auntie," even though she was only a distant relative.

Dinah brought the two children's chairs down from the attic, sat with her beside the stove, and taught her how to knit. Loop after loop wove together onto her lap, loop after loop. The yarn followed behind as obediently and softly as ever, as in the days she had crocheted the table linen; and as she had done then, when she had sat in her girlfriends' houses, she raised her voice in song.

After all, the year of mourning was already over, and anyway, who says that people sing only when they're happy? Every once in a while the door of the nearby synagogue creaked, and when she heard the squelch of footsteps in the mud she imagined that Barukh was about to come in, and it was time to get up and take the supper out of the stove.

She sang "The Orphan Girl" and "Song of Yearning"; then she hummed the song about the man who had wandered off from his warm nest and, singing it, she felt around her an icy draft and the piercing sorrow of a leaf-strewn autumn road.

At seven o'clock the schoolboys began to pass by, the reflections of their lanterns flickering on the dark wall opposite like a flock of golden sheep. In her father's house, this was the hour you felt some relief. The room would have been swept after the schoolchildren had left for home, and her sickly father would be sipping his milky tea and listening to her littlest brothers going over the weekly Torah portion:

The waters were upon the earth; and Noah went into the ark, he and his wife and his sons and his sons' wives with him. Even the beasts and fowls came two-by-two, man and wife, man and wife.

Before going to bed she went out with the maid to the hall to close the front door, catching a glimpse of the washbasin of water with its cold dark sheen, and when she lay in the dark with her eyes open she imagined she saw desolate fields, blacker than black, and Barukh with his bundle was trudging through them, just he and his bundle, alone in the world.

When finally his footsteps were heard in the yard on Friday, she burst into the hall and there, between the cellar entrance and the ladder to the attic, she laid her head, her orphaned head, still warm from her ritual bath, on his chest, and he, taken aback by the purity that emanated from her, lightly pushed her away and took off his shoes before entering the room.

Half the Sabbath was given over to God, but Barukh devoted Sunday entirely to the house. In the morning, he and Dinah would arrange the bundles of flax in the shed, and then the two of them would brush their Sabbath clothes clean in the twilight of the bedroom, and finally, toward evening, they would sit in front of the glowing stove and tie bundles of kindling for the whole week, by which, as they decreased, she would later count how many weekdays were still left.

Again the Sabbath came and erased the week's torture, and so the weeks went by.

During the eight days of Hanukkah the men of the family didn't go out to the villages, as they normally did, and on the first day of Shavuot there was a wedding in the family, and again the men went only to the villages nearest to town.

Dinah was the bridesmaid. As she walked toward the wedding canopy the candle in her hand kept going out and then she would relight it from Barukh's, and her face, which was raised toward his, caught his smile as the wick of a candle catches fire from the flame beside it.

Now Purim was virtually here, and then—the preparations for Passover, when time so easily melted away.

A week before the holiday the storm windows were taken out for cleaning, and the house was filled with a powerful whiteness and seemed to expand.

The ice on the river below the meadow had broken up, and as you scrubbed the windows, you could see over the windowsills how the river swelled angrily there, still raging at the floes carried along its current, though on the banks, a few people were already dunking their new dishes and gentiles from up the hill were netting agile pike, with their straight backs and scales merrily flecked with gold.

Dinah snipped the dry twigs off the houseplants and added to the pots black soil from the garden, which seemed blacker in contrast with the freshly whitewashed walls. She changed the colored paper on the lampshade and the corner shelves, and, for herself, to have something new to wear in good health on the holiday, she bought a cotton kerchief embroidered with silk.

Then came the sacred eight-day festival with its rest and visits back and forth and the renewing of bonds between people. For the midday meals the women prepared plum compotes and matzoh kugel with raisins, which went very well with the men's special holiday hymns, and after the afternoon nap, as evening fell, people went out in groups to pay their holiday visits. The alleys were still muddy, and the wealthier men of the family wore rubber galoshes, which added to their air of importance. When it came time to cross the puddle in the marketplace, people lined up before the plank crossing and held hands, and that was how they got across, in single file, which from a distance looked like a long chain.

The first day after the holiday was a Wednesday, so the day turned into a weekday bridge between Passover holiness and the holiness of the Sabbath. The tablecloths were removed, but in the kitchen the fine flour was already being sifted for challah, and barley and broad beans were being prepared for the Sabbath stew.

Barukh put a few leftover matzohs in his bag for his gentile friends, and before he set out for the villages he found the time to hoe the garden again, which had been fertilized from the slop bucket all winter long.

Dinah swept the yard and washed down the bench that stood in front of the house. Alone again now, she sat on the doorstep, or at the open window, where the breeze rustled through the leaves of the plants. Yes, look, they had already sprouted new shoots, and these shoots were stretching like fingers to cling to the rungs of the tiny trellises.

As the day grew feeble, Liebka the orphan came over and stood with her legs, which were still pale from the long winter, in the "windows" of sunlight that lay across the floor. She seemed to have grown over Passover from all the holiday treats, and when she lay down to sleep under the blanket, it looked as if she were taking up all the room in the bed.

The next morning they awoke to the sound of the early service in the synagogue across the alley, just as a big sun was rising. Frost still covered the ground, and the water carriers went down to the well wrapped in their heavy overcoats, but in the bakery the bread was already being baked on a bed of river reeds, and from the meadow rose the tremulous, peaceful notes of the shepherd's flute, carefree, full of spring.

Every once in a while there were spring showers, with their

first slow rumbles of thunder, long enough so there was enough time to say the blessing as they rolled. The river below would darken and the flock in the meadow would huddle together and suddenly seem as if they were fewer. The older sheep, more experienced in life, would stand stolidly and patiently, but the lambs would plunge about bleating bitterly until the old shepherd would open his coat and take them under his wing with a father's compassion.

The doors to the schoolhouses already stood open all day, and during the recess the children would come to wander around outside. They were of all ages and grades. The boys in the Bible class, the boys in the Hebrew class, and the boys in the beginning Aleph Bet class.

From time to time babies were carried in festive groups to the synagogue. These were the days of counting the Omer, and no engagements or marriages could be performed, but circumcisions were celebrated as usual—and there were many, many of them. A dense circle of adults would form around the newborn, and the baby's cries would pierce the circle as if penetrating the walls of a fortress. If he was one of the family of Beardites, Dinah would put on her satin dress and join the group right there, in the alley. As she approached, the circle would open and she would be drawn in and fall into place like a link among its fellow links.

And so the days passed.

Machla, Avner's daughter, Barukh's sister, had just given birth to her third child, and Musha too had given birth, to Basya, her eldest, and then to Chana-Esther, and then she gave birth again to Machla and Lieba, twin girls, for whom she came to borrow the children's chairs from Dinah.

"You don't need them, after all," she said, meaning only well, and looked at her from under her heavy lids. And Dinah picked up a rag and wiped down the chairs, on which there was not even a speck of dust, and then she stood watching the large woman hug them tight to her chest, one in each arm the way she carried the twins.

Shloyme, Barukh's grandfather on his mother's side, had named his only son Levi-Nathan after his wife's father, who had lived in another town, but the boy grew up to look just like one of the family: he had thick hair, an easy temper, and his face was adorned with a silken black beard that fluttered in the meadow breeze when he crossed the yard, for their house stood at the end of the street and beyond it was only the open meadow stretching out into the distance—dazzling in summer with its brilliant greenery and in winter with the glittering snow.

Because he had a foot ailment, he couldn't go trading in the villages like the others, so his father had taught him the black-smith's trade and had also built him a forge at the top of the yard with a door that faced the road. At night the flickering blaze within it could be seen all around, even from a distance. The carriage drivers coming home from the railroad station found their bearings by it, and the poor wayfarer—seeing it eased his terrible loneliness.

Right there, on Sabbath afternoons in the summer, the whole family would gather round and sit on the grass in the shade of the pear tree by the fence. On the other side stretched the open meadow with its birch woods and, further down the slope, ran the river, whose murmur could be distinctly heard now that the hammer was silent.

To distinguish among the children, they were called "Little Zevil," "Big Lieba," and "Machla the Twin." An armchair from the room of Levi-Nathan's mother, Sarah-Feyge, was carried out to the yard for old Shloyme, and Levi-Nathan himself would lie on the broad bench because of his poor health, sipping sugared water mixed with medicinal tonics and playing with his son Zevil, whose mother had died young.

After the Friday afternoon bath, Levi-Nathan's face looked eerily pale against the dark beard that framed it, and the people near him spoke in slow, carefully modulated voices and waved their hands to chase the flies from him, and the air itself seemed to breathe compassion, mingling with the odor of the Polish doctor Pavlovsky's drugs.

When his son Zevil had grown a bit older, old Shloyme would sit down with him there to test him on what he had learned, and the boy's ears, beneath his dark hair, would redden under his grandfather's affectionate pinches. He was bright, a quick learner, and he moved up from class to class as effortlessly as if he were skipping from garden bed to garden bed.

By thirteen he was already helping his father in the forge, learning Torah on his own in the evenings. Sarah-Feyge, his father's mother, had made him a linen apron that tied in the back, and after work she would bring him river water that was still warm from the setting sun so he could wash up, and the smell of the water, scented with willows and rushes, would later waft over the pages of the old holy book.

Now Levi-Nathan could rest for an hour in the afternoon

in his mother's spacious room or in the nearest birch grove. When his condition worsened, they spread out a sheet for him under the tree and covered his aching limbs with fallen leaves, warm and healing leaves, like words of comfort on a broken heart.

How restful it was, how restful, after twenty years of standing on the hard, unyielding ground.

His mother, sitting at his side, would fan him with a scarf, the leaves would rustle softly overhead, inviting sleep, and he would drop off to the striking of the hammer, as regular and precise as a newly wound clock.

He died that spring, one Saturday night, just as the pear tree had begun to bloom by the fence outside, and the river downhill was sounding its deep, full murmur. After "Blessed is the Righteous Judge" had been recited, people went to sit on the bench in the corner of the yard, and they wept for a long time, the hot tears of a close family.

It was old Shloyme who taught young Zevil the laws of mourning and who also comforted him, and when the year of mourning was over, he married the boy to one of the orphan girls who had grown up in his house, and after a year, she gave birth to a son, who was named for the dead man on his circumcision day. A wise and spiritual smile illuminated the old man's face as he handed the newborn back to his father at the end of the ceremony, passing along, at the same time, this verse: "In place of your fathers shall come your sons."

Big Musha, Barukh's sister, once went to visit her sister Machla in the nearby village of Kaminka, and she took along Avner, her baby, who was so small that he was still carried around on a pillow. The girls stayed home: Basya, Chana-Esther, the twins Machla and Lieba, and little Rachel-Leah.

Basya, the oldest, was supposed to look after them all, and each of them was supposed to keep an eye on the others, and Dinah was also asked to come over, and she arrived early in the morning, after washing with her good soap for the occasion, and the scent of the soap, along with the morning sunshine, filled her with a mischievous mood and the delicious anticipation people feel right before a holiday. She found the day's loaf of bread on the kitchen shelf, and as she sliced it, she sent sparkles through the air with the flash of the ring on her finger, which the girls caught with their joy-filled eyes. She gave them cheese and a slice of onion for breakfast, and for lunch she reversed the order and gave them the onion first and then the cheese.

When the house grew too warm, they went outside to play in the rectangle of shade beside the fence.

First they played blindman's buff and Dinah was "it," and the children sneaked away one by one until she was left alone, stumbling blindly around, but after that, when they played "colors," the children crowded around her in a tight circle. The little girls, when they tired, dropped to the ground and leaned against her, their heads drooping in her lap like the sleepy vines curled around the stakes of the fence, and she—above the worry lines on her face her eyes misted over, and as she sat like that, restraining herself and yearning, it occurred to her that she could take one of these girls as her own. The kindhearted Musha certainly wouldn't refuse to give her a child, and it was only right that she agree, for why should she have to bow her back under a precious burden that was too heavy for her to carry while the other woman walked around as if someone were scolding her, her idle, empty hands, as many people thought, making absolutely no contribution to the world?

When Musha came back that evening, Dinah tried to express her desire to her. She did not mention any names nor did she suggest when or for how long, but the big woman seemed to understand her and even shed a silent tear, and later that night she thought it over as she lay in bed.

"It wouldn't be forever," she said to herself, "but only until God took pity on her. And God may have pity on her very soon, after all, and besides, her house isn't so far away, if you go by way of the slaughterhouse. But it can't be Basya, the oldest, because how would the others manage without Basya? A hand without a thumb," she found the appropriate analogy. "She's the one who watches over them and she's the one who shows them the way. And it can't be one of the twins either, because they won't be separated; they're two pans of a scale held together with a single beam: touch one and the other pops up. And it can't be Rachel-Leah, the youngest, because she's too young. Who's going to understand what she's trying to say? Besides, her father loves her best and she's the first one he asks for when he gets home from the road."

"Then it has to be Chana-Esther," Musha decided. "She's lively and has a sweet disposition. We could even get her a pair of shoes with buttons for the autumn. But she's shy and won't eat in anyone else's house. Besides, she's frail, frailer than the others, and gets a cough as soon as winter comes." Her resolve already weakening, Musha raised herself up to look over at the little girl in the bed she shared with the other girls, and she saw that the blanket had slipped off her—and her heart throbbed.

Stirring, the child caught sight from the corner of her eye of her mother standing over her, as mighty and sheltering as God, and she smiled sleepily. And the large robust woman reconsidered, her whole body trembling with emotion.

"How could anyone send her away?" she asked herself. "Who would make sure she was covered at night if she didn't have her mother there to look after her?"

The wife of tall Avner from the hillside alley was known as "Wide" Basya—because her body was broad, but also because of the all-encompassing moral authority she had staked out for herself in the family circle. Of her ten children, she had sent five away from home, and they were dispersed throughout the town. And she had brought five brides home, all of them from the extended family: Musha, Lieba, and Machla.

When these women had children, and the house grew too small to hold them, extra rooms were built in the yard, with large windows, and when the windows were opened in the summer, the voice of that woman, their mother-in-law, would come piercing through, a shrill voice, which, like a scalpel, was generally directed at the sorest spot.

She hadn't been born in town but was the daughter of an itinerant preacher, one of those they called a "foot soldier of the Torah"—a poor man who had no money for a dowry, but he did come from a learned lineage, and he had a powerful gift for midrashic interpretation, and his daughter had learned from him to speak with rhetorical flourishes, and at family gatherings she loved to hold forth—like her father from the pulpit—while all the others were reduced to listening in submissive silence.

Because of her poor health she couldn't visit her relatives' houses, but she always knew well enough which way the wind was blowing there—the way a barometer can gauge the weather even when it is kept indoors.

When Dinah was brought to her father-in-law's house—Wide Basya baked her richest cake, as a token of approval of the newcomer's illustrious pedigree. When three years had passed without a child, she sent one of her daughters-in-law to pay her a visit; at the end of five years, she came herself, armed, as the importance of the occasion warranted, with the ancient umbrella she had inherited from her father, and which in her hands took on the form of a chastising rod.

She chose Sunday for her visit, since Barukh was also home on that day, and as soon as she came into the house, she made her way directly to the armchair, which was reserved, as everyone knew, for honored guests, and while the two of them went about finding something for her to prop her feet on, she looked around her, unhurriedly but with purpose, like someone vigorously passing a dust rag over every surface in the room.

She quickly assessed the doily on the sideboard, mentally fingered the wall hanging with the foreign proverb embroidered on it, examined the photograph on the wall of the group of Dinah's girlfriends, and finally noticed the cat, which, as she knew, was being raised in the house with everything her heart desired, and which was now leisurely stretched out on her mat as if she were a human being, and at the sight of her, Basya blurted out, in her rebuking preacher's voice, "Varmint."

The "varmint"—the woman grew angry at her when she didn't move, and Basya raised herself up now and poked her with the tip of her umbrella until the startled animal bolted and only then, when she had already reached the doorway, did the cat turn her head and take the measure of the woman with her round, wide-open eyes, gazing at her with utter contempt.

Dinah brought in a tray of pumpkin seeds and some cherry juice, and was about to take the pot of stew out of the oven, but the guest had to leave now, she was supposed to go over to old Shloyme's house. She'd just take one peek into the bedroom, "which has all that empty space," and the kitchen, "which is much too clean." She casually tapped the family-size pots that stood on the shelves, unused, and finally she made her way out, leaving behind her a mood that, she felt, perfectly suited the state of affairs in the house.

As she walked out into the street, she took another look at the front of the house and at the garden in back, a fair-sized plot, which, if it had belonged to another family, would have been fertilized all winter by generous quantities of household slops, and she could almost see the family girls, the daughters, peeping from behind the flower beds, stocky Liebas and Mushas, with heavy braids, for whom husbands would have to be found around here, if they weren't to be sent off from the shtetl altogether.

She mentally rehearsed what she was going to have to say to the hard-of-hearing Beardites, who became even deafer whenever anyone mentioned separation and divorce, and when she saw Shloyme's house from afar, and, yes, she could see that the chandelier had been lit, a sign that the more respected members of the family were there, she headed in that direction with the purposeful energy of yeast about to ferment a great mass of dough.

One day soon after, Dinah traveled to the provincial capital, to a holy man who lived on its outskirts, to obtain his blessing.

In the unfamiliar city, she bought herself a silk kerchief to cover her head, and somewhat flustered by its rustle, she made her way to the edge of the city, to the home of the wonder-worker, which was filled with sacred murmurings and the smell of ancient parchment—and all the way back in the train she tried to shield herself from the breeze, as if she were worried that some of this smell would be blown away.

She never let go of the large orange she was bringing back for Barukh, wrapped in its special paper. At home, she managed to do the week's laundry, on Friday she baked a new kind of cookie like the kind she had seen at the hotel, and when Barukh arrived, she handed him the pocketknife she had bought for him in the city, and he took the orange and cut it right to the core, and looking down at her, he laughed the hearty deep laugh of the Beardites.

As the wonder-worker had instructed, Dinah added an extra Sabbath candle to the two she was already lighting, a third, symbol of the triple braided thread, and also at his bidding she pulled her kerchief lower over her forehead, and now the girls of the family had to stoop to look at her, which they did with a silent anticipation that she met only with a kind smile.

"Be among the humbled that do not humble," the holy man had taught her. "Hear them shame you but do not respond."

And that was how she was.

She already knew how to absorb curses without complaint from her stepmother's house, and now she faced them all like a plant in a raging storm, which however hard the rain might lash, would still prove a blessing.

Machla, Barukh's sister from the village of Kaminka, moved back to town, and one of the first things she did was to come over and put her brother's house in order.

After all, standing water will eventually turn brackish and foul. She brought the dilapidated cabbage tubs up from the cellar, aired out the straw mattresses that had grown stiff with disuse and finally brought the oak cradle down from the attic and washed it in the yard, out in the open, and as it stood there drying, it rocked, in the breeze, on its own.

In time, people began to wonder whether anything would come of that man's blessing. Wide Basya even cast doubts on his holiness, since she had never heard his name in her late father's house.

Because of her poor health she didn't often visit her relatives, but in the synagogue she sat right at the center of the long bench, where her words could carry in all directions.

Once, during the Torah reading, she told the parable of a barren tree in an orchard whose owner decided to chop it down, since it provided him with nothing but a few fallen leaves all year long. She vividly described the way it stood among the fruit trees and how it was chopped down, and as she spoke, she waved her palm so vigorously that Dinah, who was standing nearby, shrank back, as if the hand held a weapon directed at her.

From the men's section below Barukh saw her pressed tightly against the railing, and he thought that yes, it must be that the bench was too crowded. But when he tried to make the others there understand that another seat had to be found, they asked him: What did he need all that room for—his heirs, maybe? So he did not speak up again.

At home he took off his satin caftan and sat staring at the Sabbath table, and Dinah, who was seated opposite him, saw only his sullen eyelids and felt as if her world had turned dark.

From now on, she prayed at home on Sabbath, beside the window closest to the synagogue. Barukh pointed out the prayers in their order and turned down the pages to mark them, and she would read from the prayer book silently, like Hannah before she had Samuel, of whom it was said that "only her lips moved, but her voice could not be heard," and she wiped away any tear that threatened to fall with a corner of her kerchief.

On Passover, after the storm windows had been taken out, the cantor could be heard leading the prayers before the Holy Ark. The children's "Amen, may His great name be blessed," was sweet enough to make her shudder.

Again it was springtime in the alley, and the ground, warmer now but still crumbly to the touch, now swarmed with children. The smallest among them, those who had been born that winter, gazed wide-eyed at the wondrous world, with their mother's smiling face at its center.

Holes in the garden fences were fixed and every day a flock of sheep came down the mountain on the sloping path. Khvedor, the old shepherd, had died and his son Petka took his place now, and he played the same old familiar tunes on the flute he had inherited from his father.

A chilly wind still blew in the evenings, and in the synagogue they had not yet finished counting the days of the Omer, but the air already carried the delicate scent of summer fabrics and the sugar cakes being baked for the shtetl weddings.

From the provincial capital came a wedding jester, who delivered pithy homilies that made people cry, concise parables with a clear moral, at the "seating of the bride." The ceremony would be held in the synagogue courtyard under a smooth satin canopy, stretched out above like the vault of the heavens, and it was usually the strapping girls from the family of the Beardites who held the canopy poles.

There were three such eighteen-year-old Liebas, all the same height, with similar builds and features, who looked so alike that it was only by the colors of the ribbons in their braids that it was possible to tell them apart. On ordinary weekdays they went out in cotton housecoats with simple colorful headkerchiefs; but for family celebrations they would shake off their sloppy ways and don muslin dresses with velvet sashes, tearing up the floor with their ankle boots in a giddy dance.

One of the three, the orphan girl who had been raised in old Shloyme's house, once burst through to the table at a wedding meal and dragged Barukh away from the seated guests, to the unconcealed delight of the women of the family. Whirling around and around him, she drew him into the circle of dancing girls, Liebas and Mushas of her own age, who formed a chain, their arms linked, spinning and changing places in a dance that made the onlookers dizzy.

Dinah, who was standing there at the side, groped for the nearby wall for support, and the smile pasted on her face flickered like a flame on damp firewood. Being short, she was easily pushed to the back of the crowd, among the wallflowers, and even so, no one paid any attention. Now she was outside the chain, a link that had been wrenched from its place.

There is a measure of sorrow the poets call a "cask of tears." It is an open vessel that collects the essence of pain, drop by drop, filling as a person's sorrow grows.

I once thought it was something like the bucket that stood under the dripping rainspout, but then I was reminded of Dinah, the year of whose divorce had arrived, which was the tenth year after she had first come to live in her husband's house. Hers were actual tears, and they flowed so freely that, as she sat on her doorstep wearing the kerchief that obscured her face, they seemed like rain falling steadily from a cloud. And there was, besides, a stormy wind blowing, the kind people don't like, which was another reason they hurried past without slowing down.

And, really, who likes to see somebody crying over things that should only bring joy: children playing in the sun, a young girl singing over her embroidery, the smile of a mother bouncing a baby on her knee?

As she planted the vegetable seeds in the garden that spring she cried, and when she went out later to weed, she cried again—with every stalk she pulled up. It may be that she was comparing them to herself, who would also soon be uprooted from her spot to make room for others.

One day she called over one of the three Liebas, the orphan girl, and told her the names of Barukh's favorite dishes. She taught her how to make a compote with honey and how to spice up a kugel with cinnamon, and then she showed her where the radishes and carrots were kept in the cellar and the rope of onions in the attic, and finally, when the girl had gone, she threw herself onto the rug between the two beds and moaned, the moan of a wounded animal in the wilderness.

And winter now arrived and with it the day set for the divorce, and she recovered and went about making the necessary preparations without further tears, and only the lines under her eyes deepened and took on a strange color, something like the darkness at the bottom of a well that has run dry.

In our house, which was the community house, there was no joy on a day when there was to be a divorce. It was called a writ of excision—my father felt—because it cut one soul off from another.

As usual, he ate no food that entire day. He had stayed up the previous night over his books, checking the correct spelling of all the parties to the divorce, considering and reconsidering all the case law on the subject of divorce.

The sages of the Talmud, as we know, had divergent opinions on this matter. When later I looked into their teachings, I could imagine which of them my father had favored. Kind as he was, he must have inclined toward those who condemned separation, like Rabbi Eliezer and his followers. The vivid story about the altar in the Temple, yes, even the altar, which sheds tears for a divorced woman certainly touched him. On the other hand, though, he might also have considered the night of that wondrous vision, that ancient night when God led Abraham outside—and the chill breath of barrenness that blew when the man asked his piercing question: "Oh God, what can you give me, seeing that I shall die childless!"

When the scribe arrived at dawn, he was told to bring over

his implements after the morning prayers, and he brought them all: the parchment, the ink, and the pen—a stiff reed, which had a peculiar, evil expression at its tip.

The divorce ceremony proceeds in a manner spelled out in the law books: the witnesses are summoned, the writing implements are handed from one party to another, and the divorcing husband is questioned, and he is always addressed, as are all the other parties involved, in the most direct form.

For the locals this was something of a spectacle, and they nearly always looked forward to it eagerly. In the cities, I later saw special buildings where people came to watch imaginary tragedies, but here the human suffering was the real thing, and the more suffering there was, the greater, usually, the demand for a seat.

For Dinah's divorce, the house had already begun to fill up that morning. By the time the witnesses were questioned at the table, all the benches along the sides were already occupied; when the husband was called up, a path had to be cleared for him through the assembled crowd.

"You, Barukh son of Avner," he was asked. "Are you giving this divorce of your own free will?"

And then, for a moment, there was an anxious silence in the room. The woman, standing still, stretched one arm out in a groping gesture, like a blind man who senses an abyss nearby, and the old beadle came to the husband's aid.

"Say 'yes,'" he instructed him.

"Yes, yes," the man stammered in embarrassment.

But the old man insisted:

"Say 'yes' only once."

And then he responded and said "yes"—only once.

After this there was some sort of commotion in the room. One of the Beardites tried to open a window to let in some air, someone else called out "Water," and from the benches in the back of the room one of the neighbor women was taken out to the kitchen.

Finally the beadle asked the people to settle down, since the scribe had begun his work, and silence reigned in the room, broken only by the squeak of the pen on the parchment. When Big Musha burst into tears, she was hushed and led to the other side of the partition, where she sat with her baby bundled on her lap, a little girl with large eyes, who, after freeing her hand from the swaddling cloth, stretched it out to her mother in a gesture of enormous understanding, and the mother kissed it, each finger separately, large and silent tears rolling down from her eyes.

I have already mentioned the cask of tears, and the way it measures, as it were, a person's portion of suffering. If it overflows and mercy prevails, that is known as divine providence or a miracle, and the custom is to recite a blessing over it, or perhaps record it for posterity in a book. For those adrift at sea it comes in the form of a hand or a board floating on the water, for those trapped in a fire—in the shape of a window, or a break in the wall; here it came in the form of a single letter, which was written improperly and sticking out of its line.

The old scribe didn't immediately understand what had happened and tried to set the dangling stroke back in its place, and then my father put out his hand and raised the parchment and before the awestruck eyes of the people was revealed a letter, from which one end had been cut off, like a limb amputated from a living creature, and it was bleeding ink and darkening like a wound in the middle of the text.

Big Musha came over to the edge of the partition, and from everything that was going on she was able to gather only that the divorce decree had been invalidated and would not be written again, because people had decided to call the whole thing off, "and it's a good thing, too," she understood, "that's the way it should be."

The image of her brother's house arose before her, with the bundles of pillows lying there on the floor and the naked furniture stripped of its slipcovers, and she stood up and pushed her way into the crowd and found Barukh with his exhausted face entirely drained of blood.

"Give me the key," she said, "and I'll go light the stove."

She swaddled the baby again and went to bring fresh milk to her brother's house and cakes "that are easy on the stomach after a fast." After that she lit the stove, unpacked the bedding, and put the slipcovers back on the furniture and finally, when she heard the couple approaching, and by then it was already dark, she lit the lamp and set it on the windowsill where it would cast its light directly toward them as they came, and then she left with the baby girl tucked under her coat, her little head poking out like a branch sprouting from a tree trunk.

Either because of her poor health or to ward off the evil eye, Dinah did not go out very much that winter, and when she did go out she wrapped herself in a huge shawl that hung on her body in folds that concealed her secret, but when summer came, she could no longer hide her joy. The "Uncle," old Shloyme, was the first to be told of her triumph, and he, in his simplicity, showed hardly any sign of surprise.

"She reached her limit of suffering," he said, "and God took pity on her."

Lieba the orphan was sent over to help around the house, and she accepted this with simple gladness, doing the housework alongside Dinah and, later, also looking after the boy she had given birth to—a big boy, in whom could be seen, from the moment he was born, the strength of his grandfather, Avner son of Zevil, after whom he was named.

Deserted Wife

It would usually happen on an autumn day. Outside a chilly rain would be falling, an ugly drizzle that penetrated right through the doorways of the shops, seeping into the woodshed and the potato cellar.

The few dark and bald trees by the town doctor's house stand trembling, and the bucket hanging from the well in the center of the marketplace drips heavy drops into the puddles as it sways back and forth on its hoist. Gloom.

But suddenly a traveler appears on the path that leads to the train station, a man with his stick and his bag, a small pack tucked under one arm. The path, in fact, is in terrible condition, a muddy bog, but it doesn't matter:

This is no traveler who rides by carriage and requires a well-paved road, this man, but just a poor wayfarer, an itinerant preacher, who trudges along on back roads, and under his arm only the single small pack.

As he passes the row of shops he pauses, takes a purse from

his pocket, and buys himself a little snuff. The shopkeeper fills his horn snuffbox for him generously, right up to the brim, and as the Jew, the stranger, feels around for some coins, he leans on the stick before him and asks him for news of the shtetls around these parts.

The preacher's only sermon will be delivered this very day between the afternoon and evening prayers.

The teacher of the youngest boys, who is staring through the window stupefied with boredom, follows him with his gaze until the courtyard of the synagogue and then sends his pupils home early, even before the sun has begun to set.

"Like cool water for a tired soul," he thinks a little later as he slogs, pale and narrow-chested, across the wet, muddy market square.

In the domed, stingily heated synagogue, the change is immediately perceptible, even before afternoon prayers begin:

Instead of the small lamp hanging over the table in the western corner where the men study the daily Talmud page, the caretaker is now preparing a different lamp, the candelabra before the Holy Ark—a gift of the wealthy manager of the nearby estate.

Into the synagogue stream not only those who are punctilious about praying in the proper, communal setting. Also arriving are wagon drivers with sunburned faces, stranded at home until the roads dry up; the blacksmith from across the bridge, and the boyish tailor who sews ladies' dresses.

The door opens and closes and then opens again. The large cotton towel flutters as it passes from hand to hand, and the water periodically splashes into the copper basin with a new, different melody.

As the service draws to a close, the caretaker drapes the community prayer shawl over the pulpit, climbs up on one of the lecterns, and lights the chandelier.

The large windows instantly darken. The single memorial candle dwindles and its glow fades. The engraved letters, "I set God before me," radiate, looking bright and freshly scrubbed, high over the Ark, and into this transformed space the melody begins to hum and surge—still muffled, uncertain, and somewhat hoarse, but nonetheless familiar and touching.

King David, of blessed memory, comes and takes his place in the Tractate of Berakhot, he and his sweet harp, which plays of its own volition, and "strike up the lyre and harp, the morning is astir"—he is strong as a lion, rising before daybreak, his spirit overflowing in prayer.

Then come:

Aaron the Priest, the pure-hearted peacemaker, with his flowering staff, the almond staff, and the bent Jeremiah, stooped beneath his burden of troubles, whose entrails contract and eyes fail from all his tears, and he seeks out a lodging place in the wilderness.

The Congregation of Israel is living in agony, afflicted, oppressed, tormented: "Every head is ailing and every heart is sick." Each day brings a new evil decree. "We were pursued to our throats. Our enemies opened their mouths against us"— the excited preacher takes out his handkerchief and mops his brow—and the congregants see, rising and turning: the double chin of that bloodthirsty government official, the inspector, tormenting them as he carries out his inspections of their shops; the drunken shouts of the gentiles and the terror of the riots on their feast days, the market days.

But rest assured: God will not abandon us forever, He will not forget us, the Holy of Israel.

"Fear not, Jacob, nor be dismayed, Israel, for I am with you"—consoles the prophet in his sobbing voice, thick with phlegm—and the darkness outside the windows seems to lift a little and it no longer provokes such terror.

True, exile is bitter and difficult, but—it is temporary, like a harvest hut in the vineyard, like a shed in the melon patch. And those who speak on our behalf do not remain silent:

From the Cave of Machpelah our Father Abraham rises to defend his children, pleading on their behalf. After him Isaac with his great terror appears and Jacob, the master of the smallest detail:

They are here for us, they are here.

Our Teacher Moses complains, his voice trembling: Can this be true?

And King David does not hold his tongue either. If need be, even Mother Rachel herself makes an appearance.

Swathed in light and cloaked in mourning, she raises her hands from afar, her compassionate, motherly hands, weeping bitterly as she walks, rending the heavens with her pleas, so powerfully that the Holy One, blessed be He, can no longer restrain himself and withdraws, as it were, into a corner and sobs like a baby.

And here begins the main event of the sermon, the explanation, and the illumination: the parable.

Once upon a time there was a tender young princess who married a king. Her husband loved her dearly, and had canopies and beautiful textiles woven for her and gave her precious jewels and pearls, and did not leave her side until he had a golden gown made for her. Then one day the king grew angry with her, stood up and demolished the canopies, ripped off her jewelry and clothing, and then left her and sailed off to a land across the seas.

The neighbor women gathered around her, shaking their heads, and saying: Woe is this poor woman, for what her husband has done to her. And there she sits desolate, her hair unkempt, writing her lament through the night to bemoan her fate, crying her eyes out—the preacher lowers his voice and leans on the podium, and the congregants below crowd closer to the platform, and all around people stand in silence, with bated breath.

From afar, on the western wall, comes the sound of the clock ticking off the minutes one after the other, and in the chandelier, the full flame trembles and hums the secret song of its light. A hush.

Above, in the women's gallery, semi-darkness reigns. A ray or two of light penetrate the letters of the stained-glass Mizrach plaque and fall diagonally across the walls, onto the tiled stove and the charity box of Rabbi Meir the Miracle Worker.

Close beside these stained-glass letters stands a solitary listener—the wife of Reb Raphael the rabbinic judge, who had come in at sundown to say the "Kaddish" and "Barkhu" prayers.

Her small head, bound in a black cotton headdress, is cocked a little to one side and rests against the wall, and her two eyes are riveted to the mouth of the dear man, who's standing right there at the pulpit below.

The biblical verses and rabbinic sayings are meaningless to her, though, and stick uneasily in her mind, like the stale bread in her husband's house that scratches her toothless mouth. But it's alright: she has her sock and ball of yarn with her, and she's here anyway, getting her knitting done.

She switches the knitting needles from hand to hand every once in a while without counting stitches or checking, without even looking at them: she knows how to knit by heart, just as she knows the "Kaddish" and "Barkhu" prayers that she has come to hear.

But now the preacher adjusts his prayer shawl, bends over to lean on the podium. He has reached the climax of the parable—and the woolen sock drops from her hand along with the yarn and knitting needles:

The fate of the desolate abandoned woman strikes deep into the heart.

Poor, tempestuous woman, woe is her and woe is her life—she shakes her aged head back and forth. A bitter, salty bile rises in her throat, a sort of mirror of the abandoned princess's tears, and in her eyes glints the age-old sadness of the woman who has been robbed of justice.

And the preacher continues to speak all the while, swimming steadily onward, onward.

After the parable comes the moral with its proofs and re-proofs from the Prophets and Writings:

Where is the bill of divorcement of your mother whom I sent away?—sayeth the Lord.

For—the Lord has taken you back as a wife forlorn and forsaken. Can a man cast off the wife of his youth? For a time I forsook you, but with vast love will I bring you back.

Again the melancholy melody, soft and somewhat hoarse, but now a trace of exhaustion is perceptible within it and the impulse to tie up the loose ends, to plow with one last burst of strength to shore.

The large clock high up on the wall rings seven times with a clear tone that is full of warning:

The time for evening prayers has arrived.

One of the congregants coughs, then another seconds the motion. The preacher gathers the fringes of his prayer shawl, lashes together the verses with force and power, and slides downward in one swoop, as if on a mountain slope.

And "a redeemer will come to Zion, speedily and in our day"—he pushes the podium aside, removes his prayer shawl, and begins to fold it.

They rush through the "short Kaddish," their voices dry, and then come "Barkhu" and the "Shema." The whispered "Eighteen Benedictions" and a quick spit at the mention of idolaters in "Aleynu"—and then, when the first person opens the door, the cold damp bursts in from outside and blows workaday grit on everyone's face.

The caretaker, after setting the lecterns back in their places before the benches, lingers a little longer before the Ark, trimming and straightening the wick of the memorial candle and climbing up to extinguish the candelabra.

The room suddenly darkens. And the shadows across the walls stretch out and quiver.

Upstairs, only a single pale ray of light penetrates the women's gallery, trembling and wavering to the prayerful rhythm of the candle before the Ark below. Every time the door closes downstairs, up here the windowpanes shudder, the copper lamp in the middle of the ceiling sways, the solitary, shabby flower tucked into the kerchief of the wife of the rabbinic judge trembles.

She, the old woman, has already rewound her yarn and set it on the bench along with the sock, but she has not yet relinquished her place by the lattice. Time and again she cranes her head to the partition, her eyes searching among the men leaving the synagogue, and everything, her quilted housedress and striped apron, her whole worn-out body spells uncertainty and dissatisfaction.

Only after the preacher himself has left does she move toward the stairs, and only as she descends, only then does she remember that she left the sock and ball of yarn upstairs, on the bench—after all that she goes and forgets them—and she sighs and climbs back up the stairs to retrieve them.

In the cramped, dimly lit house she moves about back and forth for a long time in the narrow space between table and stove, scrubbing and washing the pots and setting them on the shelf face down. Finally she takes the black headdress off and replaces it with a simple white cloth, laying out the bedding as she whispers the bedtime "Shema," and then she gets into bed.

The space, as she puts out the lamp, darkens. The scurrying of the bugs coming out of their holes can be heard now, from the potato cellar rises the smell of rot, a damp smell that's not so good to breathe, like the smell of the ancestral stones in the graveyard outside town on autumn mornings, and the old woman, turning her face toward the window, stares out at the night peering in from outside and remembers how the preacher compared it before to the darkness of exile.

For a few minutes she lies motionless, her eyes shut, as if

she were ready to fall asleep. But now a sudden tremor shakes
her heart, passes through her entire body, and the bitter, salty
bile rises in her throat again, as it had in the synagogue before.
And the sadness she had felt at the end of the sermon suddenly
becomes perfectly clear to her:

The "princess."

And then she collects herself, turns over slowly to look toward her husband's bed.

"Raphael," she stretches a gaunt hand through the air. "You
understood what he was getting at, there, in the synagogue:
What happened to her? What happened to the deserted wife?
Did he come back to her, the husband? Did he come back?"

There is no reply. He, the old man, is not asleep, but he does
not answer.

"That's what they're like, always," she shakes her head, as it
were, to the fairy-tale princess, gesturing with her head that
she means "them," men, and then she turns back toward the
wall, toward the window.

The house is suffused with a damp chill and the smell of
rot, a damp, moldy smell, and the night that peers through the
window from outside is dark, very dark.

Shifra

Shifra had light eyes and dimples in her cheeks, and her complexion was so clear and delicate that just for that—people figured—it was worth it for Pinchas the cabinetmaker to court her for three straight years and then marry her without a dowry or even a proper wedding dress.

Later, after this Pinchas had died, and she, left with two children to raise, went back to her mother's house, two or three curls at her temples turned white; the azure of her eyes also dimmed and grew murky from her tears, but the radiance and delicacy of her face remained unspoiled; and her mother, a sickly woman who spent her days by the stove, as she looked over at Shifra, melancholy and captivating, nursing her child, would think that "with only a little luck, God willing," even now Shifra could put all those plump girls with their rouged cheeks to shame.

And this thought was directed to her neighbor's uncle, the wealthy and tall shoemaker, who had so yearned for Shifra a few short years ago, and who now turned his eyes to a seam-stress in the provincial capital who sewed him cloth shirt collars as gifts.

Pinchas had died, after a brief illness, at the end of the Sab-bath, before they could light a candle in the room, while the men were still standing in the dark synagogue at their evening prayers.

That very morning he had been asking for the pillow to be plumped and the curtain on the window opposite to be drawn, because he wanted "to see the world"—he said—and by eve-ning he was lying on a mound of wood shavings, and some of those very shavings were taken to heat the stove so that water could be boiled for the "purification" ritual.

Someone carried the two children wrapped in a single shawl to the old woman's house. For lack of a new cloth for a shroud, the best sheet was taken from the chest, the one that had cov-ered the workbench on holidays.

Shifra hurried after the shrouded body on its stretcher with her mouth open, but unable to utter a word, as if she were dreaming, and she was heedless of the slippery ice that covered the frozen puddles, also as in a dream—and when after that she awoke at first light in her mother's house, she was stunned by the new paleness that lay across the walls. On the other side of the unshuttered windows could be heard the shriek of crows, and large flakes floated soundlessly through the gray air—the first snowfall.

It will cover the grave—the thought sliced through her heart like lightning and brought tears to her eyes—the same tears that first saddened and then dimmed their blueness.

And the snow fell, fell, fell without stopping.

In the Semianovka forest the wood trade came to a halt. At the risk of life and limb, from across the river Jewish peddlers brought a few potatoes, which were sold by weight as in big-city stores, and only the strongest of the water carriers could break the ice in the well, after scraping the snow to the side with their buckets. The Sunday church bells wailed mournfully across the white marketplace, which lay desolate, without the stamp of a horse's hoof or a merry voice, under sagging clouds that dropped, with no respite and with desultory stubbornness, more and more snow.

At night the dogs howled from across the river. The rafters in the attic groaned under the weight of the snow—and the Semianovka farmers looked like sleepwalkers as they sank with their wagons into the snowdrifts by the river crossings while, across from them, on the other side of the river, their fellow villagers struggled mightily to make their way to them, rescue poles stretched out in their hands.

One morning, after the goat had been up all night bleating with hunger and in the house the last few little grains of semolina for the baby had run out, Shifra agreed to take in some laundering from one of the houses.

"The skies are clearing now," she said, "and I can make my way down the street by walking in the water carriers' footsteps."

Because she had no other coat, she put on her late husband's, a short sheepskin jacket, which fit her, incidentally, and suited her, too, immediately absorbing the young widow's charm in its folds, and the old woman, her mother, helping her tie the ends of her kerchief, went out to the yard after her, atremble with a final hope, to see whether someone might be peering out, as in the olden days, from the neighbor's house.

But the shoemaker's window, alas, showed nothing but a dark, sullen reflection in the crack between the shutters, although the stove that had been burning inside there all day long had completely melted the frost from the windowpanes.

Among the tools on his workbench proudly stood a high-heeled shoe, whose metal hooks seemed to be entwined, so closely did the two rows lean against each other, but the shoe tree had not yet been removed—that would be done when the young girl from the city came for her fitting—and the old woman bitterly made up her mind, and when the agent's wife appeared again with her idea of sending Shifra off to the estate as a wet nurse she put her off no longer; she only tried to argue that the two-month-old baby be allowed to accompany her.

"Since he isn't eating any food yet," she said, "and as for his mother's milk and disposition—if only her luck were so sweet."

Nevertheless, on the following day, when the lady herself came in her carriage from the estate to negotiate, these arguments struck even her, the old woman, as pointless.

For even the two horses outside the window waited importantly, and the lady radiated that glow of wealth as she entered, while here in her house it was dark, as dark as only a poor house can be on a cloudy, chilly winter's day.

The creeping mildew on the leaking walls, the sooty stove right by the door, and finally, the large washtub that stood there right in the middle of the room, overflowing with dirty laundry.

The honorable woman showed signs of impatience as she spoke, and pulling a handkerchief from her fox fur muff, she began fluttering it in the air around her, at which point the agent woman stood up and intervened in the discussion. She suggested that milk could be sent from the estate for the two-month-old baby.

"Since the goat here is not producing milk," she said, "and a little milk would hardly be missed over there, what does she say, the person in question, Shifra herself?"

And Shifra, who had been sitting off to one side all this time, the baby who was the subject of these negotiations on her lap, smiled an embarrassed smile with only her dimples and said not a word.

She was silent as well on the morning that followed, sitting in the master's carriage on the way to her position on the estate.

To keep the chill from penetrating her body, the old woman had tied a rope around her jacket at the hips, and the ends of this rope, along with the edges of the jacket itself, peeked out with trembling puzzlement from under the velvet cover, which was fastened together with two clasps.

There flickered the slaughterhouses outside town; windmills with listless arms, sunk into the snow up to their bellies; telegraph poles, on whose cables a few birds swayed, their feathers bristling.

In the village of Semianovka, on the right, a church bell was already ringing across the great expanse of snow and at the sound of this ring, Shifra hunched over and shut her eyes, and with the swaying of the carriage and the pinpricks of cold, her own body seemed to her insubstantial and lost, a lonely bird by the roadside.

Where was she being taken? And how could she have forgotten to swaddle her baby before she left? She drew her neck into her shoulders, as birds do, and her baby's blue eyes looked at her as if through a fog, miles away. Then the old woman, her mother, appeared, lifting her ravaged face to her for a kiss, and finally her husband, Pinchas, in his cabinetmaker's apron, gazed at her from the distant horizon, stretching out his glue-streaked hands toward her.

But here the warmth of a cowshed was blowing around her now, and there was a smell of abundance, of a granary, and dogs were barking, and before Shifra had managed to shake herself from her reverie, she was lifted down off the carriage and hurried off to a large foyer, within whose darkness, between rows of coatracks and potted plants, she found herself suddenly face to face with her own reflection in a mirror.

She walked along the slippery floor without stumbling, as if she were dreaming, for what seemed like an hour, through winding hallways, with the draft blowing down them from both directions, and dogs gathering at every entrance and door along the way.

The bath in the washroom, without steam, without the commotion of the bathhouse, reminded her of the hospital in the city where she had been taken years ago when she was ill, and where the nurse, businesslike in her uniform, had stripped her naked in broad daylight, just like the maid who was standing now at her side.

"You should try to put on some weight," she advised her, and clad only in a shift, having been told to put on only her shoes, she was brought to the next room for a medical examination—and the feeling she had in the hospital never left her after that.

In another room, beside an open closet, between two mirrors facing each other, they put a flannel dress on her and a small frilled bonnet suffused with some strange fragrance, and then she was given hot cocoa to drink in a special, enormous mug, and finally, after the new mother had looked her over for herself, under the watchful eye of the doctor, a tiny creature was brought to her chest, who fell upon her with a drooling mouth, a strange heat, and a new thirst she had never experienced—the thirst of a bloodsucking leech.

And then it happened, as she was going to her room in the stillness of dusk by now, that a sobbing moan suddenly broke in her throat.

She was passing through one of the darkened parlors with a glowing stove in it when she heard from afar, from the direction of town, the tolling of the evening bells, and that was when the moan rose in her throat, and since she could no longer find the door because tears were blinding her eyes, she sank right down onto a sofa, beside the row of embroidered pillows arranged on it. The maid, who had come in to stoke the stove, warned her to stop it.

"No good, sister," she said, leaning on the poker in her hand, with no apparent surprise at the tears, "they like good spirits in a wet nurse, and now look at you—crying. You get up, take a walk outside, cheer yourself up or something. Main thing is— hold back, hold it back."

But Shifra could no longer restrain herself by any effort of will. Curling up against the pillows on the side of the sofa, she sobbed, a lost sob, aloud, no longer hearing the coaxing of the girl, who approached her in despair and gestured that there was no longer anything to be done, and that she was in for whatever she was in for.

And indeed: from behind a screen at the opposite entrance appeared the wealthy master of the house with his son, a student who was visiting from the city, and behind them came the husband of the new mother and the heavy old lady, who was forbidden any excitement by the doctor's orders—and in fact there was nothing more that could be done, really.

The maid, catching her breath, could now hear her own heartbeat, so quiet had it suddenly become as the lady bent over, lit by the fire from the stove, to pull Shifra off the splendid sofa.

Alas, she dropped to the ground, the way an old, worn dress finally drops, without making a sound as she fell.

"No, no, no, no," she shrieked with a terrible hoarseness, drenched in tears, stubborn and ungrateful from her head to her toes. And with no worry about upsetting the new mother, or waking the infant, who no longer had a wet nurse since "that woman's" milk was now deadly poison for him, the lady ran shouting at the top of her lungs to the furthest parlor, despite her doctor's warnings and the midwife's pleas to have mercy on herself and refrain from getting angry, since her health was at stake.

Just a little hint of a tear glistened in the rich master's eye, as his wife, pacing the carpet, described the torments of the negotiations in the shtetl, in that suffocating little house, over the children's wails and the shrieking of the goat.

And after all that—the whole series of preparations: a bath, a medical examination, a complete change of clothing, and . . . the hot cocoa—her voice by now had grown clear and a flash of sarcasm lit her face—and then the doctor seized the moment to present her with a tranquilizing draught in a cup.

And the new wet nurse who was brought the next day had to undergo the entire series of preparations again: a bath, a medical examination, a complete change of clothing, and finally, the hot cocoa, as well—from the special mug, the one that had been set aside in this house from time immemorial for wet nurses.

In the face of this substantial villager—a girl who had just dropped her first child, a baby who had died only two days before "of unknown causes"—Shifra felt insignificant, and she seemed to herself frail and terribly short when her low-heeled shoes were returned to her, and without waiting another moment until she could find the carriage, just tightening the rope around her jacket for warmth, she went out a side entrance to look for the way back home.

The driver, who had brought her yesterday in the carriage, acted as if he did not recognize her and quickly disappeared as she approached the stable door, but the shepherd, the milk-woman's son, hurried to show her to the gate, and at the sight of his blue eyes under his sheepskin hat, walking and piping on his flute, she felt as if a sob were about to burst from her throat, the way it had yesterday.

But the wind was at her back now, and there was the smell of abundance, of the granary, and dogs barking, and Shifra, cutting across the lane of acacias, hurried toward the gate, after which the way would be marked by the tread of the winter sleighs.

From time to time she had to close her eyes against the

snowflakes falling on her face, and then there flickered before her the gigantic mirrors in the manor house, the copper pots on the kitchen shelves, and the broad hands of the village wet nurse poking like talons from their soft flannel sleeves.

Not very far from town, as she sat down beside a dilapidated bridge to rest, a kind of deep sleep fell upon her, and from within the webs of dreams that caressed her, the azure eyes of the two-month-old baby gazed at her again, as they had during her carriage ride. Then the Semianovka farmers appeared in a long line, walking tall through the snowfields with their rescue poles in hand, and after them, in a cabinetmaker's apron—as radiant as on the day he was told that she, Shifra, was willing to become his truly wedded wife—came Pinchas, walking steadily toward her to greet her.

How strong he was as he approached to save her from the clods of ice. How could anyone imagine that the shoemaker, their neighbor, was any taller than he, than her Pinchas. As she lifted her head, she smiled at him, the charming dimples deepening in her cheeks—and that was how the farmer from Semianovka found her, by the side of the road, at nightfall, burrowed deep into her jacket, while her head, tilted up a little, leaned against the bridge post.

The blue that glistened between her eyelids was as bright as if it had never in her life been touched by a tear.

Grandchildren

Sarah Basya, a skinny old woman with a light step, is wearing her Sabbath headdress today and her gaily striped pinafore fans out around her like a banner as she walks:

"I have a mazel tov coming to me, our Barukhl began putting on tefillin today," she says.

"Whose Barukhl?" they ask.

There are more than a few Barukhls among her grandchildren, since that, after all, was the name of her father-in-law, may he rest in peace, Reb Barukh.

"Chana's, from the butcher's lane," she answers, moving off down the street.

There, in a small house as old as she, the blind old man waits for her, sitting at the table before an open Talmud, "perusing" it as he learns from memory.

He senses the approaching footsteps, recognizes them, and his face, framed by a white beard, lights up as he turns toward the door.

"Which of them were you visiting?" he cranes his neck to inhale the special fragrance she's brought with her, the smell of grandchildren.

"May the evil eye keep away from them," she ties a linen apron over her dress and begins setting the table. "They pounce on me and yank my sleeve or my pinafore string: Bubbe, give us candy, Bubbe, give us nuts, Bubbe this, Bubbe that. And our Zalman, two teeth have poked out already." And the old man washes his hands, makes the blessing over the bread, and sits at his place:

"May he live to be a hundred and twenty." His face turns pallid. "And the bread, Sarah Basya, needs to be softened in the soup," he says.

They eat their meal peacefully, the two of them from a single bowl, she tearing off pieces of bread to dunk in the soup, and he taking out his handkerchief from time to time to mop his brow, his eyes:

"It almost smells like honey dumplings here," his nostrils flare.

"You're dreaming," the old woman tries to bluff, and from the rustle of the silk ribbons on her headdress, he knows that she's laughing.

"Nu, nu, come on," he pleads. "Be an angel, Sarah Basya, tell me."

"So who do you think could have sent those?" she's already wavering.

"Chana, from the bar mitzvah?"

Sarah Basya is silent.

"So then it must have been Hodl: leftovers from the engagement party."

But no, because Sarah Basya doesn't answer, she doesn't chew either, since her mouth is too busy laughing. He puts his hand to his forehead, thinks for a minute, and then all the wrinkles spread out across his face as he takes up his spoon again:

"It's Benjamin, that's it, they're about to have another Barukhl there," he grins victoriously and approaching the golden honey-covered balls of dough only to smell them, he puts them back on the sideboard for the children and goes over to the couch to lie down. Sarah Basya, when she has finished washing the dishes, draws the pleated lace curtain across the front of the stove and, putting on her glasses, sits down beside the window with a sock.

Silence. The right half of the room, the one with the better furniture, had been straightened that morning and the burnished copper tray dazzles. An old clock ticks. Paper flowers are displayed on the corner table, the granddaughters' handiwork, and above them, arranged in a triangle—the glory of the house—is a group of photographs:

The elder daughter, Michele, from the provincial capital, beside a table, among potted flowers, with a small grandson on her knee. Leybl the watchmaker, the American, in necktie and tails on his wedding day, beside his veiled bride. A grandson, a high-school student, his head bare and a book satchel over his shoulder; and a large-headed baby with a stunned look on his face, propped up on a chair, two hands grasping his shirt. And over them all—a family portrait:

Shmuel Dov and Sarah Basya, he with his rabbinic sash belted around him, and she in her pinafore and lace headdress, holding hands, and around them, as if from the trunk of an immense and sublime tree, branch out—according to Sarah Basya's instructions—the descendants by generation: sons and daughters, sons-in-law and daughters-in-law, and their sons and daughters, sixty-two people in all.

Three naked babies, fat and curly-haired, float like small wingless cherubs above the heads of the group—the great-grandchildren. The grandchildren brought two of them from the city when they all came last month to be photographed. By now they must have two or three more teeth and know how to say Papa and Mama.

"Our Jacob went to the city," the old woman announces from the window. "I'm sure he'll visit the children there."

"Oh, Jacob?" the old man rouses himself. "It's time our Jacob married off his youngest already," he declares. "Then we could have another great-grandchild."

And now, at last, the family start to arrive.

In comes Jacob's daughter-in-law with a baby in her arms, Mirl from the dry-goods store with the twins, and the miller Shloyme's daughter from across the bridge, at the smell of whose clothes, the smell of reeds, flour, and the river, the old man pulls himself up to sitting and stretches out his hands as if to say, "Come closer, that I might feel you."

"Feygele?"

Now the old woman removes her glasses and puts them away, along with the knitting needles and everything else that's sharp or pointed, and goes over to the sideboard for the honey dumplings.

From Benjamin's nearby store they send over a tray with glasses of lemonade and a letter from Senderl, from the county seat, that has just arrived with the post, and which Feygele, twelve years old and a bookworm, sunburned and serious, reads aloud.

Things are sometimes tiresome and sometimes go smoothly, there are ups and downs, very much like life itself.

"Wheat prices are flat out dead this year, but on the other hand the demand in the city for lambskin and linseed is booming. I should also let you know that my Golda gave birth to a daughter and we named her Rachel, like our grandmother Rochele, may she rest in peace"—Feygl plows through the letter forcefully and then with her slender finger marks the place on the page where she was interrupted until the storm of joy around her simmers down; tossing back the curls from her face, she sighs deeply.

When the reading ends, the clamor in the room that had been stilled rises in an instant to its former intensity. Sarah Basya lifts the lace curtain and opens the stove to take the kettle out for tea and, getting the little ones out of her way, the old man starts to entertain them.

"They're going cheap, they're going cheap!" he cries. "A pair of Moisheles for a single penny." And his baby great-grandson, barefoot and warm, is suddenly lifted high, his shirt riding up, and using both fists to grab hold of his beard, he folds himself into his grandfather's body. A flush spreads over the old man's cheeks. Clutching the soft body to his heart, he nuzzles him, stroking him and burying his face in him, as he tenderly calls, from the depths of the baby's soft belly, to his wife.

"Come over here, smell this and you tell me," he says. "Huh? Isn't this just the most heavenly smell?" And as the old woman approaches the couch, the little one opens his two blue eyes, raises his head, and coos:

"Dji, dji, dji."

And every corner of the house fills with laughter.

With nightfall a deep hush comes over the house. Toys, nut-shells, jacks, and small stones are strewn across the floor and the old man stands girded in his sash beside the window, be-tween the dresser and the couch, praying. The lock on Benja-min's store squeals; someone is closing the shutters there from outside, and Sarah Basya, with her old woman's trot, cuts across the street to bring the goat, who is home from pasture, into the shed.

"Nu, I have to go, Shmuel Dov," she announces, and from the festive tone in her voice it's clear to him that she has news. And then, turning his face to her without interrupting his prayer, he asks—in the Holy Tongue:

"A male child?"

The old woman slowly takes off her good coat and pinafore, exchanges her lace headdress for a plain one, and a smile spreads over her face as she remembers that they already have honey dumplings for the celebration.

What perfect timing, the dough had been rolled into balls and fried that very morning.

Returning home after midnight from the "vigil," waves of sleepiness wash over her before she can even finish the bedtime prayer.

"And lead me not into humiliation or tribulation," she mur-murs, confusing the morning and nighttime prayers, and sinks into the pile of pillows, and images mingle and float before her eyes along with the flicker of the lamp that just went out: the face of the young bride in childbirth; soft, nearsighted Benjamin, the wrinkles on his face showing his age; Mirl from the dry-goods store; and Gisha, old Aunt Gisha, stooping over to the ground in her holiday clothes to light two candles.

"What, candles? Why is she lighting candles on the ground?" Everything suddenly falls away beneath her, and for a moment, between wakefulness and sleep, she sees, as if through a veil—a pitch-dark abyss. But then a ray of light penetrates the house from outside and trembles and dances over the dresser, the copper tray, and the group of photographs arranged on the wall: Benjamin is descending to the ice cellar, his mother-in-law Chana lighting the way with a lamp.

Are they bringing up some milk for the new mother? she wonders, feeling better, as she grips the verses of the bedtime prayer again. And after that, turning to the other bed:

"Shmuel?

"Listen: during the intermediate days of Succoth," she says, "when the children come from the city, maybe we should take another picture?"

"Mm? Another picture?" the old man rouses himself. "We're sixty-four now, with the two new ones."

"For the moment we're sixty-four," the old woman replies, the ground beneath her solid again. "But our youngest daughter is going to have some news for us soon."

Ziva

Ziva came to live in the courtyard in the middle of the summer after her owner had moved out and her owner's husband, the man who was always glowering, had let her know that she was no longer welcome in his house.

"He threw her out, the brute," Ghazal—the cook from the apartment across the way—put it in no uncertain terms, "just like he did to his own wife."

From her kitchen, which always stood open, she couldn't help but see his "fine ways," how he would seethe if some girlfriend would come over to visit the woman or when, in her spare time, she would tend to her plants.

"And once, when they were eating," she whispered to her friend from the top floor, "he threw his lunch smack into her face, the poor thing, the meatballs and then the plate right after it."

Ziva, had she been endowed with human speech, could have

told them a whole lot more. More than once, after the man had left in the morning, she saw her owner bury her face in a handkerchief or lean her head on the windowsill or the arm of a chair and silently sob.

Her hair, which hadn't been brushed yet, had slipped out of its bun and fell loose; she would toss it back while still clutching the handkerchief to her eyes. Meanwhile, Ziva, crouching at her side, would tentatively lick the hem of her dress or the limp slipper dangling from her foot.

"Go, go drink, from the bowl, there's milk in there," her mistress would say in a broken voice, and, doing as she was told, she would lap a little milk and then lie down again until the greengrocer arrived to hawk his wares at the gate, when her owner would rouse herself, wash her face at the sink, and go out with her shopping basket, trying to look happy.

"Good morning, Mrs. Berg," the elderly lawyer from the second floor would greet her.

"How are you?" chimed in the engineer's wife, who had also come down with her basket and, bending over Ziva, she slapped her affectionately on the back.

"Your dog is getting prettier by the day," she said.

"Yes, my Ziva is getting prettier," her owner replied, putting on a cheerful face.

Afterward, in the kitchen, she would tie on her apron and go over to the burner—and soon the copper basins on the shelf and the aluminum pots reflected bluish, glowing flames. The water from the faucet splashed happily from time to time, the vegetables in the saucepan bubbled merrily, only she, the lady of the house, moved among them sad, pounding the mortar in the pestle with efficient hands and then turning the handle of the meat grinder while, from time to time, drying her tears with her apron.

When the clock struck two, she would hear the sound of his heavy footsteps on the path outside and she would go into the dining room and set the table.

"Now you go sit in the small room," she would warn Ziva.

You see, he had no use for Ziva. He would glare at her through his thick glasses whenever he happened to notice her, and sometimes he even ground his hobnailed shoe into her paw, obviously trying to hurt her.

Her owner would then come and stroke the place where it was sore and the pain would go away.

It was amazing how the touch of her hand could soothe any hurt. Even taking a bath in the washtub, which Ziva hated, became sweeter when it was her hands doing the washing.

In the afternoon, the doorbell would sometimes ring and a woman with a heavy tread, also wearing glasses, would enter.

"That's his mother," Ghazal informed her friend Naomi from the top floor, "a truly revolting woman."

Inside the apartment the woman went to bring tea from the kitchen and cakes and fruit from the pantry and laid them out on the table, maintaining her friendly expression.

"Isn't your dog here?" the guest peered at her with a malicious glint through her glasses.

"No, she's not here right now," the woman replied.

She peeled the fruit and set it in front of her, and stirred her tea for her, all with that same friendly smile. Afterward, when her husband and his mother had gone, she went into the small room, stood by the window facing the street, and shed silent tears. And so it went until the night a loud thud was suddenly heard in the apartment and her owner burst out the front door onto the street with a wail, while she, Ziva, in the small room, scratched at the walls in the dark and tried in vain to find a way out.

When she left the room the next morning, the house was already empty. The large flowerpot lay broken on the kitchen floor, clods of moist earth around it. Nearby, beside the sofa, were her owner's slippers, muddy and somehow cowed. All astir, she licked them and went to look through the other rooms.

She heard the greengrocer at the front gate, and then someone knocked on the door. She presumed, from the smell of the fresh bread, that it was the boy from the bakery. Finally, the key creaked in the keyhole and hoping, anticipating, she ran to the entrance, but oh no, it was him.

He overtook her with two strides as she turned to escape, flung her up in the air with his foot, and opened the door for her.

"Boy, do I despise you," he said, flashing his rage-filled glasses at her—and he pushed and shoved her outside.

Ziva, picking herself up, first sniffed out the courtyard.

She peeked into the storage shack, went down to the cellar, and then climbed up all three floors. She pushed the door to the roof open with her head, then stopped short, startled by the radio antennas turned toward her like whips trained for a lashing. Finally, after she had gone back down again to the courtyard, passing between rows of wash that blew a damp chill on her, she went to huddle beneath a bush near the spigot and sat whimpering faintly, in the same tone of voice her owner had been recently using.

"Who is that bawling over there?" the lawyer from the second floor asked his wife angrily; he'd been wanting to catch a nap after lunch.

The frightened woman went down, intending to scold Ziva, but at the sight of her loyal dejection, she relented and just tapped her lightly on the head.

"Quiet, sugar," she said to her in Hebrew, which was the language Ziva knew. "It's time to sleep now."

"She's crying for her owner," retorted Ghazal from the nearby balcony, whispering, because her boss the pharmacist was also about to take a nap.

And she went down to pick up Ziva and set her on the balcony, getting a little porridge and milk for her.

"Eat, you poor thing," she coaxed her as she put the dishes on the stairs. And to Naomi, her friend from the top floor, she said:

"After all, she's practically an orphan now, got no master, no one to take care of her, no one to even say one nice word to her. And that's what really counts, you know," she went on. "You can take any sort of pain if only you get a little kindness, like the way Mama and Papa used to give you. Because then it's like the sun is shining on you. You don't feel the cold, the pain can't get you, you can bear anything they throw at you. You just don't care."

She pulled a sack and some shavings from one of the cartons from her boss's pharmacy, fashioned a sort of mattress, and put it underneath a bush, and that's where Ziva spent her first night out of doors. But she was constantly bothered by stinging ants and drops of water that splashed on her from the nearby spigot.

Once, late that night, she imagined her owner's voice calling her. It came from the street, a muffled and frightened call. Approaching the gate, she stood on her hind legs to throw herself against it and then, suddenly, the window opened above and there, in his pajamas, stood the man.

Ghazal, when she came toward her the next morning, did not recognize her, so much had she changed in the course of one night. Her bright shining fur had dimmed, and burrs dangled from it. Her eyes were murky and bloodshot.

The dentist's little girl, who played with her on the grass every morning, now pushed her away in disgust. "You're filthy," she said to her candidly. The plumber, who had come to fix the water pipe, he too gave her a nasty look: "Whose doggie is this?" he asked.

"Mrs. Berg's from the apartment across the way," Ghazal hastened to answer. And to Ziva, who had pricked up her ears on hearing her owner's name, she explained:

"It's not good for people to know that you don't have a home anymore. People don't like that kind."

After lunch, she once again gathered the leftovers from the meal and put them before Ziva, coaxing her to eat while she washed the dishes.

"She doesn't seem to have much of an appetite," remarked the engineer's maid, who was waiting near the spigot.

"That's because she's eating her heart out," said Ghazal. "When bad things happen to human beings, at least they can talk about it; but she—poor thing—has no words."

And she asked the maid not to throw away any leftovers

from her kitchen from now on but to put them here, under the bush, instead.

"You certainly don't need them for your own dog," she said.

Lucky had a special dish prepared for her every day in her owner's house. Meat with rice or cereal, and he, the engineer himself, took care of her grooming. He washed her in the bathtub, combed out her fur with a special brush, and polished the brass collar around her neck with his own hands.

"That's how it is when luck is on your side," Ghazal said to Ziva, who looked over, from the corner of her eyes, to the balcony where the two of them were sitting now.

"You know, the two dogs are sisters," she told Naomi, who was also gazing in that direction.

"Lucky and Ziva?" the maid couldn't believe it.

"From the same mother," she answered. "They're only a year apart."

"Then why is that one so big and black and this one so small and white?"

"Because one looks like her father," explained Ghazal, "and the other like her mother."

One day, when Ghazal went out with Ziva to the courtyard entryway, they were both startled to see the man coming toward them along the path. Ghazal, holding the edge of her apron, had wanted to cover her companion, but she immediately saw that the thick-lensed eyeglasses were trained solely on her.

He was asking if she would be able to wash the floors in his apartment.

"Maybe," the girl answered with relief. "Why not? If you leave the key for me, sir."

After she had finished her work at her own boss's house, she took the rag and bucket and gestured to Ziva to follow her.

"Don't be afraid," she said, when she saw Ziva hesitating. "You can see with your own eyes that he's not here."

She opened the door of the apartment across the way and entered while Ziva followed behind, her whole body taut and her ears alert.

Nothing was visible in the darkened corridor but a mirror through which you could see the doorway and a short apron hanging alone on the coatrack. The girl paused beside it, stroking it softly and exchanging a meaningful glance with Ziva.

"Yes, that poor woman," she said, looking at the fine stitching along its hem. "She must have brought this from her mother's home."

She gently pushed the kitchen door open with her foot and then stopped short.

"Damn him, that bastard!" she exclaimed at the sight of the broken shards of the pot, with the clods of earth strewn about. "This is her ficus plant, her favorite plant that she brought from home. She used to carry it around like a little baby when she first arrived, taking it out every day to get some sun—without fail, come summer or winter."

While she was talking, Ziva went around sniffing the chairs and the tablecloth on the table, paused for a moment beneath the clock, listening attentively, and was about to push open the door to her owner's room.

"It's locked," Ghazal said, after trying the door. "I guess he doesn't want anyone going in there."

She went into the nearby room with her, on the floor of which lay a small mattress with an empty bowl at its side.

"This must be your little bed," she said. "And over there is the window where she would stare at the street—always so sad. If someone came by outside, she'd put on a happy face. But her heart, you could tell, was sad, always sad."

She went into the bathroom now, took a rag and some water, and washed the floor and watered the plants on the balcony, and then, as Ziva gratefully followed her around, she took the little ficus plant, to which clods of earth were still clinging, replanted it in a pot and, amazed, watched the plant start returning to life as the water seeped into the earth around it.

"Did you see that?" she said as she placed the plant on the wooden pedestal where the woman would always set it. And stretching herself upward, Ziva leaned against the rail with her front paws and licked the large kind-eyed girl's shoulders and braid. Then they went down to the path and turned to go to the house across the way, walking side by side, united by the same stirrings of the heart.

At the end of the summer something happened at the pharmacist's home that indirectly affected Ziva's destiny:

The family rented an apartment closer to the pharmacy.

They were supposed to move that very week, so Ghazal put her mind immediately to the task at hand, which she knew would be a daunting one, because her masters, like those of Joseph in Egypt, left her to handle all their possessions, and with her at hand, concerned themselves with nothing beyond the bread they ate.

She began with the glassware and china, which filled the cupboards to the brim, and had to be packed meticulously. Then she went on to the draperies and valances, whose intricately embroidered fabric and complex system of hooks and clasps only she, who had always tended them, could fathom.

At the same time, she designated one hired maid to organize the linens and another to polish the copper, and she was the one who supervised them. She would run to the pharmacy from time to time to bring paper and packing twine, and in the midst of all this, she did not neglect to warn Ziva never to go out the gate without her because now she was homeless again and needed to watch her step.

Once, as she returned loaded down with coils of twine, she reported that she had just bumped into one of Mrs. Berg's friends, who had told her that the poor woman had gotten really sick after her divorce, but now she was recovering little by little.

"Yes, yes," she said to Ziva, who rose and stretched when she heard her owner's name. "Don't worry, she'll come and fetch you yet."

The next morning, a large moving van stood before the front gate, and the movers began loading the furniture out of the pharmacist's apartment—mostly through the windows, since the doorways turned out to be too narrow for that purpose.

Overstuffed sofas and armchairs appeared, gliding down the face of the building on ropes, while wicker hampers and trunks were taken out through the balcony, and it was Ghazal who orchestrated the whole operation.

Even the most ordinary wooden kitchen utensils were scrubbed by her order at the spigot, and the wash buckets and kettles were noisily dragged from the courtyard, accompanied by the barking of Lucky—the engineer's dog—from her doorway.

In the middle of all this, there suddenly flashed before the girl the pockmarked face of the bully Musa, as he crawled beneath the bush and whistled seductively to Ziva, and she, throwing aside the bundle of clothing she was holding, jumped from the balcony as if she had been bitten by a snake.

"What are you doing, you devil?" she cried. "This dog is ours, it's Mr. Stahl's, the pharmacist. I'm going to call him right now from his pharmacy," she said as she pushed the frightened boy out the gate behind him and forcefully pulled Ziva, who had meanwhile managed to run toward the wagon with the caged dogs inside, back into the courtyard.

"What am I going to do with you! What can I do if you have no brains in your head!" she scolded. "How many times have you been told that someone like you who has no owner and no tags on her neck has to be careful, and here you are, crawling everywhere.

"Why did you run over there?" she asked, stooping as she walked to gather the clothespins the movers had scattered on the way to the van, and Ziva, who understood nothing of these words except for the warmth with which they were imbued, walked right behind her at every step, rubbing herself against her legs from time to time as a sign of loyalty, or rising up on her hind legs to lick Ghazal's arm where she had rolled the sleeve up to her elbow.

By day's end, all the rooms of the apartment were bare, and Ghazal, sweeping them with a broom she had borrowed from one of the neighbors, closed the shutters and windows and then stood for a while in the dark entry hall and said in a sad, hushed voice:

"Good-bye, home."

She had spent most of her waking hours during the past six years in these rooms. She swept, polished, washed, and went crazy over any stain, any grain of sand that found its way in there.

She could still remember her early days there, when her boss and his wife would leave at the crack of dawn, and she—she was still a young girl at the time—was left alone in the apartment, scared out of her wits.

Once, during that first winter, her mother had suddenly come here. She had heard that a house had collapsed in this neighborhood, and she had plodded her way across the sands and come over. When she saw her, hale and hearty—she was in the middle of washing the floor—she held out her hand and placed it on her head as if she were blessing her. She didn't say a word, just stretched out her hand that way, and then she left, limping on her weak legs. Ghazal, finding a dry place on the floor, had sat herself down and cried.

That happened yet another time when she came back from sitting shiva, after the week of mourning her sweet mother, who had passed away, was over.

She entered the house quietly, and when she saw that the floors were filthy, she went and fetched the bucket, and then, her lady poked her head out of her room and said, "Ah, Ghazal, you've come?"

She could think of nothing to say to her, but her face had turned pale, for she really did have a good heart.

Then Ghazal went and set down the pail of water, there in the living room, sat down right on the floor, in a corner, and the tears began to flow. She sat alone in the middle of this large room, the clock ticking above, she crying below.

The movers called out to her because the van, loaded to the top, was just about ready to roll, and then she grabbed her basket and hurried to the gate, and Ziva, who was trying to join her, she pushed away with one hand.

"I asked Naomi, from the top floor, to do you a favor and keep an eye out for you. She won't abandon you," she said, and climbed up on the crowded van and squeezed in among the furniture, forcing herself to look away from Ziva, who was circling below.

Hadn't her two orphaned sisters run after her just like that when she left for work every day, and didn't she harden her heart to them and walk right on?

"What can you do?" she summed up the matter to herself. "That's life."

Days went by and everything Ghazal had predicted from the day Ziva had been cast out came to pass:

As if orphaned, she wandered around the courtyard with that feeling all too familiar to a person who's been down and out—when everyone around you suddenly fails to notice your presence. They look above or around you or, at best, they size you up scornfully.

The engineer's wife, the same woman who in the past might have given Ziva an affectionate pat on her way to the green-grocer's cart, now would look right through her, passing the spot where Ziva crouched by the bush, without registering her presence, and the bakery boy would look at her with mocking eyes as she ran up to him, barking, and laugh disdainfully.

One day furniture was delivered in a van to the gate, and movers filled the pharmacist's empty apartment again. The next day, when the kitchen door was opened and the familiar smell of cooking wafted from there, Ziva climbed the stairs in the hopes of getting a little something. But then, a maid wearing an apron came out and hinted to her that she'd better try her luck elsewhere.

Not that she had anything against her or was angry at her, it's just that she didn't want this creature, who looked homeless, coming in and out of her kitchen. And as for Naomi, the maid from the top floor, she was working too hard in her lady's house to keep her promise to Ghazal, and Ziva, when the hunger pangs overcame her, was forced to forage for her dinner in the garbage can.

Sometime around then, something happened that threw her into turmoil for some time:

In the kitchen of the new resident, the man they referred to as the "manufacturer," there was a theft.

It happened on a Sabbath morning, when the men, home from work, were sitting on the balconies dressed in their ample robes that looked like women's housedresses, and the women, since they were not going out to the market, were, by contrast, walking around in pants—their pajama pants—and busying themselves around the house, since their maids, Yemenite girls, had the day off. Then, the manufacturer and his wife appeared at the door to their apartment, also dressed that way, and started asking whether anyone suspicious had been seen in the court-yard, since a large fish had been stolen from their kitchen.

The people on the balconies hadn't seen anyone. Besides, the gate was closed, since peddlers and beggars wouldn't be coming by that day. Then the lawyer came up with the hypothesis that the dog that had been roaming around here lately was the culprit. This hypothesis seemed plausible.

The manufacturer asked if she—that one—had any owner and was duly informed that whereas she had once belonged to one of the residents, the latter had not been seen in the courtyard lately.

"Such being the case," the man said, "she must be duly punished. Otherwise, nothing will ever be safe in any kitchen."

And he went down to the courtyard.

Ziva, who at that moment had come out from under the bush, was heading for the garbage can when the man grabbed her and carried her up to his kitchen, from which, soon after, issued the sound of a beating, accompanied by yelps of pain.

Those standing near the door could see a platter on the floor, with carrot slices arranged like a wreath around an empty center, to which the man drew the dog's attention after each blow so that she would know why she was being beaten.

During this time his wife, on the balcony stairs above, was telling the neighbors about the losses she had incurred. It was a fish weighing ten pounds, and she had cooked it whole in a special casserole dish.

After a while, Ziva slunk down from the balcony and headed toward her spot, while the building on her right seethed with people in their colorful clothes like laundry hanging on the line on a stormy day.

The dentist's little daughter, the one who used to play with her on the grass, called out from the second-floor balcony:

"Shame on you, Ziva!"

Someone from that same floor plucked a few pinecones from the nearby tree and threw them at her.

Only the lawyer's sickly wife would have none of it—she didn't believe one word of the story.

"It's impossible," she said to herself, "for a creature as weak as she is to swallow a fish nearly her size." Besides, she knew her to be a good soul who couldn't even bark properly.

When her husband had fallen asleep that afternoon, she even found the courage to bring some food down for the dog.

She gathered the leftovers from their meal and placed them beneath the bush.

"Eat, darling, it's good," she said in her broken Hebrew.

And Ziva, encouraged by her soft voice, immediately got up and started to eat, lending the woman, to her satisfaction, some evidence that she had been right.

"How likely is it," she thought, "that she would gobble up some leftover spinach and barley if she had just swallowed a whole fish weighing ten pounds?"

The following night, something came to pass that the people around had been anticipating this late in the autumn, but with which Ziva, on account of her youth, was as yet unfamiliar: the first autumn rains.

Early in the evening, something like a black curtain descended on the sea horizon. Somewhere beyond the buildings, something grated and rolled as if furniture were being moved, and then, the cypresses near the fence suddenly bent over, letting out a groan. The linen drapes on the balconies waved and quivered, and fresh, tender twigs began flapping in the air and lashing the head and face.

As she always did in times of crisis, Ziva tried to take refuge under the bush, but in these gales it couldn't protect her. The bush shook in the tempest and was lashed repeatedly against the fence posts, the way you shake out a coat.

The walls of the storage shack rattled, and shutters and doors banged open and shut repeatedly. Somewhere in the distance, in the black turbulence, a demented sob could be heard. Was it the wind wailing or the lament of all those wretches, life's outcasts, with no roof over their heads on a night like this?

It wasn't until dawn that the rain ceased and the wind subsided a little, but the gutters all around continued to surge and the puddles continued to grow; in the heavens above, torn shreds of clouds ran around with angry frowns and so, too, did the people.

Ziva, by the dim light of dawn, found herself a spot in the entrance to the shack and settled down, but then one of the residents came and shooed her away, so she pulled herself up and walked on.

She was stunned, sick, soaked to the bone—so when that infamous man, Musa, came by and extended his bold, dry hands, which seemed to her to promise shelter, she walked right into his waiting arms.

The nimble man carried her through the gate and set her down inside the cage, which was already filled with the morning's hunt, and it had been a successful one. Settling himself at the head of the wagon, he moved off down the street with the same equanimity with which his friends, the garbage collectors, would drive their wagons here every day.

After all, those creatures behind him were nothing but miserable wretches with no home, no one needed them and they were a public nuisance.

Ziva, to smooth the bumpy ride, sank down and leaned against the grid of the cage. She froze in that position, motionless, and didn't move even when her name was called out, and only when this call was repeated, and the familiar tone of affection could be detected within it, did she get up and stand upright, suddenly feeling her heart expire, the way it does in those sick with longing, when the beloved appears after all hope has been lost.

The passersby would then have been able to discern a short woman on the sidewalk, dropping her large umbrella and extending her arms toward the moving wagon. Her face, the blood suddenly drained from it, was joyful and terrified by turns as she beseeched the man on his seat with such a pleading expression that even he, dogcatcher though he was through and through, capitulated and waved her over to a nearby alley, where it would be easier for him to pull over and stop. It stood to reason, he thought, that in the course of their transaction he would be properly rewarded.

Here, in the middle of this narrow alley open to the sea, the wind blew hard, and even the rain, which had stopped at daybreak, began to fall again, but Ziva no longer minded because that which the Yemenite maid, in her wisdom, had once compared to the sun, which gives light as well as warmth, was now shining upon her—that, surely, was love.

The Early Stories

Sister

As a symbol of the past—all sadness and humility—my mother's face swims up and rises before my eyes. Her eyes two black abysses, anguish peering from them; her lips moist and rosy, a smile always hovering over them.

Did she also have beautiful hair? Did she have a nice voice? Who knows? She was a modest Jewish woman who never sang out loud in her life and her head was always covered with a wig, even around her family.

A blue silk cloth embroidered with golden dots—that was what she devoted all the days of her life to. Was it a quilt for my oldest sister's bridal bed? Was she intending to decorate the Holy Ark in the synagogue with it? That remained her secret. But she did her work in purity.

Hunched over the embroidery, her gaze buried in the cloth—hours would pass with her sitting like that. And the slender needle danced between her white fingers as the clock ticked away on the wall. Only when it was time for the midday meal and Father came home from the old study hall, his brow knitted and forehead clouded, only then would my mother's grip slacken and the needle slip and fall onto her lap, and her gaze, full of both compassion and rebuke, would wander over our faces—the four faces of her poor daughters.

She had borne my father four children—and I, the youngest, was already twelve years old—and there were no sons to join my father in the blessing after meals.

We would eat our lunch deliberately and in silence. Only between courses would my father sometimes lift his eyes from his book, stretch and apologize to our mother for having arrived late to the meal:

He hadn't even gotten to the study hall today: there was a celebration he had had to attend. A baby was brought into the covenant of Abraham. He was asked to be the godfather at the circumcision . . .

"The circumcision . . . right," a stifled, half-choked sigh, and again it was silent. And when Friday arrived and the sanctity of the Sabbath hovered over the whitewashed, sunlit walls of our house, the kitchenware was scrubbed and gleaming and the beds were made—Mother would approach the table and light all seven of her large candles, covering her face with her hands, and two hot teardrops would hang in her lashes and tremble there for a long time.

Mother would pray silently, only her lips moving.

We had a grandfather in town and he too had a lugubrious face and a stooped back—my mother's father. He had sent nine daughters off to various cities, and Mother was the tenth. He visited her every day, sitting here and staring at the bookcase.

He had two such bookcases in his house, each of them with

more than a few shelves, and the Hebrew books on them were as numerous as the white strands in his beard—but who would pore over them when he was gone? He had no son.

And what was he doing coming over to Father's house every day?

In our neighborhood stood a dilapidated old building—the community cheder. From there now emerged clear voices, the voices of children learning Torah, and the old man would shake his large head, listening intently, and turn to our mother:

"And the candles for the synagogue, have you already donated them, my daughter?"

"Candles?"

And with a light step, my mother would go over to the sideboard, take out a sack of candles and tuck it into her shawl, and she would step out of the house, the old man looking after her for a long time and nodding. How much mute compassion there was in that melancholy stare!

A small boy with a cherubic face and silvery wings fluttering in the air, hovering over our house and showering us with joy, happiness, gaiety—he wasn't just something we had dreamed up. From somewhere, a skinny, long-limbed aunt arrived in our home—my mother's sister—and took over the work, frying, sorting chickpeas, and between the walls of our house could be heard the rustle of cloth, the clatter of the sewing machine: This aunt was an expert at sewing those little outfits with sleeves and collars—something like a miniature man's caftan— and a flush bloomed in my mother's cheeks.

And every evening the glasses rang on the table and the samovar hummed, and another aunt, my father's sister in her fringed wrap, stirred the sugar into her glass of tea for a long, long time:

"When the pregnant woman's cheeks are rosy—that's a good sign."

So she intoned, and Father—from where had that youthful glint in his eyes suddenly appeared, when the creases on his wide brow were already so deep? No, he no longer rushed back to the study house now. The house was so warm and pleasant and, moreover, it was full of neighbors and relatives—how could he be so rude as to leave them? No. He would stay and chat over a glass of tea, reminiscing about his childhood: Father—what a prodigious Torah scholar he had been—day and night he would meditate on the living words of God, day and night. Crowned with phylacteries and wrapped in a prayer shawl, his face was as radiant as he studied as the face of the sun and his whole form was like that of an angel of the heavenly Host, flies sizzled as they flew past the breath of his mouth, and he, my father, was only two years old and he already sat on the dusty ground at his father's feet, feasting his eyes on the radiance of his face and absorbing every word that emerged from his mouth . . . His mother, a saintly woman in a long line of saintly women—whoever had not seen her face as she lifted him on her shoulders and carried him off to school has never seen what a devout Jewish woman looks like, a woman of forty-five—and she skipped like a six-year-old girl through the streets and market to the cheder, in the evening she carried him home and her legs never failed her.

And he himself, he grasped everything quickly and forgot nothing—at seven years old he was already reading the Mishnah. And he had a gift for Talmud and could explicate difficult passages with ease—by his tenth year he was uprooting mountains with his sharp mind . . . and now came the thirteenth year of his life. In their home, in a hidden corner, sits the scribe writing out the verses of the phylacteries. Behind him stands Father himself, making sure that the parchment touches no metal and checking the letters, measuring the margins and fingering the leather straps. In the other room sits Mother, carefully embroidering a square bag of pure velvet, with silk fringes.

And one summer morning, as a bright sun shone in the sky, and his father's face cast a radiant light, all the community leaders entered the house, sitting around tables laid out for a feast and all eyes were on him, the bar mitzvah boy:

"Let's hear the sermon!"

And then he stood up and opened with the importance of the commandments and their reward. And he unveiled commentaries that no ear had ever heard before, and every phrase that emerged from his mouth was a blaze of fire, and one word chased another and one brilliant insight another—like a fountainhead—and his voice grew stronger and stronger, and he waded deeper and deeper into the sea of Talmud, diving down to bring forth pearls, linking them together, and juggling them in the air like rays of light, like sparks of divinity . . .

When his voice subsided, but his face still shone with the light of Torah and the radiance still dwelled in his eyes—the eldest of the group rose and kissed the top of his head, and all the guests approached his father, one by one, and clutched his hand: "Blessed are you, rabbi, that such a child has emerged from your loins." And his father himself embraced him and drew him close and called him: "my teacher and master," and from afar, Mother floated out of the other room, all decked in lace, the hem of her dress fluttering and rustling like the wings of an eagle and she was dancing—leaping four feet with every step, four feet with every step:

"My kaddish, ay-ay-ay-ay, the son who will say kaddish after me, ay-ay-ay-ay," so she was carried along, flying between the ceiling and floor, her hands raised high. On her ears quivered and sparkled the large gemstones of her earrings and on her eyelashes hung tears . . .

"And she, she too was rewarded with a son only in her fortieth year," my father would finish his story, turning to look at Mother.

And each of the guests would make their way home after warm good-byes, and for a long time Father would continue to speak in an intimate tone to Mother, and for a long time he would caress her with his warm gaze:

Didn't she think a fringed wrap would look wonderful on her, like the one his sister Malka had worn? . . .

It was now the middle of the summer—the three weeks of lamenting the destruction of the Temple had yet to begin, but the walls of our house already wore mourning. For two whole days and nights my mother's groans rang out in the air and for two whole days Grandfather did not stop reciting the Psalms, and my aunt her Yiddish supplications. Father—he too prostrated himself in prayer and begged for mercy from the All-Merciful, and when all these voices finally subsided, the skies over our world suddenly clouded over, and a strict and cruel silence pressed down on our house. Even the old man took his walking stick and left the house without saying good-bye. Like

the knock of the gravedigger on the graveyard gates—that was
how his stick reverberated through the floor of our house. He
never came back to visit us again, Grandfather, never. From
the bookcase the rows upon rows of books peered out, through
the open windows penetrated the mournful voices of young
boys studying Torah, and he didn't come the next day either
or the day after that, nor did he come on Friday. Only Father
now remained at home, his face screwed up in a grimace. Back
and forth. One step toward the bookcase and the second to the
sideboard. His brow was clouded; what was he thinking now?

Now he stopped for a moment beside the table on which lay
an open Talmud, fixed his gaze on the tiny letters and read for
a moment, swaying back and forth:

"Ach, woe is me! . . ."

And again he clasped his hands behind his back, and started
pacing again.

"Perhaps the dear brother-in-law might be interested in dining with us today?"

No, he wasn't, he couldn't eat a thing today.

He couldn't eat—wasn't that apparent from his pale face,
his angry brow?—so why was the aunt pestering him with her
requests?

"Hush-sh-sh-sh . . ."

What's the aunt taking those chickpeas out of the house for?
Was she returning them to the store?

Chickpeas are of no use to us now, the aunt explained with
a wordless gesture and added, to us:

"Hush-sh-sh-sh."

When did all that happen? An hour ago, maybe two—the
beadle of the study hall had come by:

Tomorrow is the Sabbath, tomorrow Father will be called to the Torah, so he had announced.

"So what?" Father had grumbled.

"The man only meant to ask if they had decided on a name for the newborn girl yet," the aunt ventured.

"The name of the girl? Hold on," and he continued his pacing. Let him just think a little, settle down, clear his mind . . .

"And the brother-in-law won't be attending synagogue to-day?"

Synagogue? No, he was feeling a bit ill—he would pray alone.

Father not praying in a quorum—we all take this in, all four girls in the room, and something tough contracts in our hearts, and stepping softly and sadly we withdraw, each to her own corner, making herself small and slinking into the shadows, and her soul weeps in secret; today is Sabbath eve and the house—its glory has departed, its radiance gone. The walls haven't been scrubbed, the table isn't set and the large lantern hangs on the ceiling cold and ashamed. Only the seven candlesticks stand on the table in a neat row. The large, burning candles within them—their wax steadily melts, dripping and dripping away. Or maybe those are tears, tears of the good angel, weeping over the departure of the Shekhina from our house? And Father hasn't even changed his clothes, he hasn't clipped his fingernails, he hasn't stopped pacing. But wait; now he's stopping beside the table, passing his hand over his high forehead, stroking his long beard and staring at the flames of the candles with a sharp, focused gaze:

"Blessed are those who dwell in your house for they will p-r-a-i-s-e y-o-u f-o-r-e-v-e-r."

No—my heart will not be moved by my mother's sobs. My sisters' and my aunts' mewling cannot tug my heartstrings—for they're women, but Father:

"For they will p-r-a-i-s-e y-o-u f-o-r-e-v-e-r, God full of mercy!" And how his lips, his shoulders tremble.

But what was that thud, of something dropping, which suddenly came from the sleeping alcove?

"Oh no! What happened there?"

It was Mother, whose fault this all was. When she heard my father's voice from the dining room she was shaken to her core and rolled herself into a ball and buried her face deep, deep in the pillow. The newborn girl had slipped off her lap, falling to the floor—so said the midwife, trembling, and the wails from the other room grew louder, hoarser, and more heartrending:

"Ay, ay, ay," I can see the little body now, twitching in agony, the drooling, toothless mouth and the flushed, swollen face, from which peek out two deep, black eyes—my mother's eyes—and on the forehead, narrow and small, a crease is already forming—and some warm and gentle stream suddenly courses through my heart, fluttering and rising within me, stopping my breath with a lump in my throat:

Poor, tiny creature, how could I quiet her? I—I don't even know what to call her, she doesn't even have a name.

And I stoop over the cradle, hold out my hands to her, and overwhelmed with pity, I cajole her, calling out to her loudly, very loudly:

"Hush-sh-sh, my little one, sh-sh-sh, my baby, sh-sh-sh, my

sister, yes, you are my sister, you are..." And God knows why—I suddenly bury my face in the tiny blanket and start crying myself.

From afar, from the dining room the softest, saddest tune reaches me—my father has withdrawn into a corner and begun the evening prayer. Outside, through the bedroom window, the evening is already gazing in.

Burying the Books

Seeing that some holiday was just around the corner and my mother's industrious hands were busy in the kitchen, scrubbing and koshering the dishes, my father would go over to his large bookcase, survey it with a long stare, and announce:

"Looks like it's time to get the books in order!"

This would just fill me up with joy. You see, I knew what getting them in order meant:

Father would stand on a footstool and crane his neck up. His eyes would be fixed on the books, while his hands were busy going through them.

He takes a book out of the bookcase, inspects it from every side, dusts off the cover, and sets it back in its place. Here's another book; this one is a little torn. The cover is missing entirely. Father leafs through the pages: they're wrinkled, some have come loose, and my father decrees:

"To the burial box!"

And immediately he puts it aside.

Now he takes a bundle of loose pages of all sizes, tattered and worn. They're covered with candle drippings, thick with dust. He quickly leafs through them:

"To the box!"

And the pile of torn pages rises higher by the minute . . .

Now Father replaces the last book on the shelf, gazes at the tall pile of books and pages. And running his hand over his wide, handsome brow, he turns his eyes on us now, on me and my brother, Shloymke.

"Okay, gang, this pile of holy pages goes to the burial box."

And we dance over to the pile:

Me, I stretch out both arms toward my brother, and he, very deliberately, takes each of the torn books, each loose page, looks it over carefully, leafs through it, and turns it every which way before he places it on my arms.

"Here's one . . . Here's two . . ."

Sometimes I feel my little arms—outstretched—grow numb from all the waiting; at moments like that, I want to throw down my heavy load and rub some life into my aching arms, to move them around . . . But to hurry my brother along a little, that I'm afraid to do:

I could remember that once, when my brother was really taking his time over each and every book, I started to plead with him.

"Come on, already, my arms . . ."

He hurled a furious glare at me.

"You're in a rush, are you?!"

And he added scornfully: "That's what I get for trying to work with these girls."

A minute later he turned to me:

"Leave them alone. Put the books down . . . go play with your dolls, go on!"

My lips twisted with a suppressed sob, something bitter choked my throat, a tear glittered in my eye.

When my brother noticed my tears he fell silent and continued loading the books onto my arms.

"Here's one, here's two, here's three."

I looked at him gratefully.

"I have a plum . . . here, if you want it—it's yours!"

Finally, the moment I've been anticipating arrives. Loaded down with torn books and pages, the two of us, my brother and I, now go into the woodshed of the old synagogue. It's always half-dark in there. We pick our way through the bundles of wood and kindling lying around, stumbling from time to time over a plank or a broken piece of furniture.

I deposit my pile of torn books and pages on a log, wipe the sweat from my face and survey my surroundings.

Well, here I am, right inside the place the boys never let us girls into . . . I walk over to the corner, where the chuppah is kept, with its satin canopy and four green poles, and how smooth they are to the touch—I caress them with every one of my fingers . . . And there, in the far corner, there's that broken lectern; two prayer shawls with missing fringes are tossed beside it. And now I see the box for the torn holy books. My brother stands there, leaning over the box, his hands buried deep in the pile of damaged books, searching, searching for something.

From time to time he pulls out some torn book, looks at it curiously, thumbing through the pages. Now a page falls to the floor and he hurries to pick it up, lifting it to his lips and kissing it over and over again.

And I can't get my fill of the sight; my face glows with pleasure, my eyes glint, and sneaking glances out of the corner of my eye at the synagogue yard, I think:

If only they'd come over here right now, those boys—I would stick my tongue all the way out to show them:

Ha! Chase me out of here now!!! Go ahead, try to chase me out!

And when I awake one summer morning, I find my father standing on the footstool beside the bookcase, handling the books. My brother, Shloymke, face aglow, eyes sparkling, has already taken his place beside him. He watches impatiently as my father's hands sift through the pile of torn books and pages over and over again.

My eyes wide with astonishment, I stand before him: "Now, in the middle of the summer?"

But I don't wait for an answer. Within minutes I'm dressed, my face and hands washed, my teeth brushed; in a flash I'm standing next to brother, who hisses at me: I'm fasting today; everyone's fasting today . . . Today—is the *genizah!* We're not just collecting them, now's the time we bring them to a Jewish grave.

And then he adds:

"Hold out your arms, hurry!"

He picks up the torn books one at a time and quickly hands them to me.

"Here's one, here's two . . . here's—what's this?"

And now he picks up a little chapbook, torn, tattered; the

pages are creased, covered with yellowish stains. He turns it over and looks at it; and muttering something, he flings it into a dark corner:

"Rag!"

I catch a glimpse of the book from the corner of my eye, and my heart shrinks:

That book—it's Mother's book of women's supplications. Those stains are Mother's tears, the same hot tears that flowed whenever she read through it.

And pleadingly, I look at my brother.

"Shloymke" . . . but he's already pulling my sleeve.

"Hurry up, it's time to leave."

And we go out to the old synagogue yard . . . here—Oh! my God!—it's packed with people, so many men, so many women, so many children! And they're all in their Sabbath finery, and everyone's face is shining. Here are the klezmer musicians, too. Yankl the fiddler stands in the middle of the throng, his fingers flitting over the strings of his violin, which tremble a little beneath his hand. Near him stands a group of little kids; they're amusing themselves with the town billy goat, pulling his tail, stroking his beard, making him stand on his hind legs, and trying to dance with him.

Two snow-white mares harnessed to a stately wagon stand before the synagogue. They toss their manes, stamp their hooves impatiently, and flick their tails to shoo away the stinging flies.

Here's my father, next to the wagon now. His face is pale, his eyes are teary, and he's staring at the entrance to the synagogue. And now, out steps the synagogue beadle, a damaged Torah scroll in his arms.

Father takes a few steps toward the beadle and bends his

head to give the Torah a kiss. He reaches for the Torah carefully, the beadle places it in his arms and Father grasps it carefully and hugs it close, close to his heart, and kisses it again.

A mother embraces her only child, as he dozes off, in just that same way. Even though it's a shame to disturb him and she wouldn't dream of waking him up—still she can't resist snatching a tender kiss, kissing him and hugging him to herself!

And now the torn books and pages are removed from their box. Many hands make light work—placing them into large barrels standing ready in the wagon.

Finally, the mares start to move. Father walks up ahead, the Torah scroll in his arms. The klezmorim strike up a melody. Young boys dance and push themselves among the adults; a boy stumbles and falls to the ground. Another boy grabs the town billy goat and pushes him into the crowd, and many voices call out from within the procession: "Women—to the side!!"

And here we are—at the graveyard.

Tall trees, black and white stones sunk in a sea of grass. Birds take flight.

Here too is the open grave, filled to the top with books.

Father is standing right by the grave. He speaks, his voice tremulous:

"Friends, today we bury our Torah scroll . . . these torn prayer shawls, these holy books . . . but do not imagine for a moment that they will stay buried forever . . . For surely the day will come . . . when our Redeemer arrives (and here Father gestures toward one grave and then another) and then . . . and then . . . we will take our leave of this place, and with us . . . we will carry these books along with us too."

And a picture unfolds before my mind's eye.

I see—the Messiah, he's really come! Here he sits astride his snow-white mare, blowing a long blast on his shofar, a long blast, toot-toot-toooooot.

And a great commotion breaks out in all the graveyards. Skeletons stagger about, dry bones rattling and shaking; and the bones come together, bone to bone, and the sinews and the flesh grow upon them and join together, and the skin comes together to cover them up. A throng of the living-dead; shrouded in white and all facing east . . . Here is my father, too; his face radiant, his eyes sparkling, the Torah scroll pressed to his heart and he kisses and embraces it, embraces and kisses it, calling out:

"Friends! Take it all, all of it! . . . all the torn books, all the crumbling pages . . . Friends, our Torah, our Torah! . . ."

Along comes my mother, too; how stooped her back is! Her face is drawn with worry. She wrings her hands and softly sighs and pleads:

"Has anyone seen . . . my book of supplications? Where is my tkhine collection? Where did it disappear to?"

My heart quakes, my brain reels in confusion. I force my way through the crowd and run home. I feel a stitch in my left side, I'm panting, dripping sweat, my curls blowing wildly in the wind—but I keep running.

Here's her tkhine. It's lying in the corner, its pages have come loose, it's covered with yellowish stains . . . I grab it and race back to the graveyard. My father is still standing there, face pale, eyes teary and lips moving.

And now I'm the one who's right by the open grave.

"Sh-sh-sh-sh! ! !"

The pages of the tkhine rustle as they touch the other worn books in the grave.

And it seems to me that those torn holy books reproach the poor, wretched tkhine.

"Filthy r-r-r-a-g! Get out of here! . . ."

In another moment my brother has approached; peering into the grave, he glares at me, pulls the tkhine out, and tosses it aside—far, far away.

A painful stab pierces my heart, my head spins . . . and the trees dance and whirl in a circle now around me and everyone around joins in the dance . . . and so I myself begin to dance, until my feet trip on something and I sprawl to the ground.

When I opened my eyes, I found myself stretched out on my little bed. My mother was sitting beside me, smoothing my curls.

I gazed at her affectionately and thought to myself.

"Poor mother! You haven't the faintest idea of what just happened, have you?!"

Kaddish

My grandmother bore my grandfather ten gifts—ten children, but, alas, not a single son. They say that every time a girl was born, he would lift his thoughtful-pious eyes to heaven and sigh deeply:

It seems, Father, that you don't consider me worthy of a son, a son who could say kaddish for me when I pass on . . .

And at nightfall, he would sit down listlessly at the table, open the big Talmud, and sadly, very softly and sadly, sing to himself. Somewhere in a far-off corner between the wall and the partition, my grandmother would sit and listen to the Talmud chant and cry in silence.

Later, after my grandmother had died and my grandfather took me in, a tiny orphan, to feed, I would often hear this very same mournful chant.

Late, very late at night, when a thick, mute darkness would press up against our little window from outside, my grandfather would light the lamp and sit down at his Talmud. All is quiet now, and melancholy. Only occasionally, from some distant field, comes a soft Hoo, hoo, hoo.

That was the wind, chasing its tail somewhere out there in the darkness, stumbling over naked fields, and sobbing softly.

And inside the house, mute, terror-black shadows would wrap my grandfather in dark shrouds, veiling his clouded-gray face, his high forehead, his deep-set, sad eyes:

Ay, ay, Father, ay, ay, sweet Father.

And it was hard to know, at times like these, whether he was thinking about himself, about his lonesome life, and crying, dry eyed, or whether he was really absorbed in the words he was chanting.

Ay, ay, Father dear . . .

"Zeyde."

And running through the shadows with my tremulous steps, I would sneak onto his knee.

"I want to listen to you learn."

And my little body would be set loose between his cold, thin hands, which stroked and hugged me, clutching me close, close to his heart:

"Ach, Rivele, Rivele—if only you were a boy . . ." And a strange look would come over his face and his eyes would become dejected and thoughtful.

What a beard he had, my grandfather, white all over.

I remember the Sabbath days, the winter Sabbaths in my grandfather's house. Outside—a disheveled, lumbering sky over the congealed, dead earth. It's quiet and dismal. Every now and then a flock of black crows flies by, hurls a few curses into the air, and then disappears, and again it's quiet.

But now the winter sky is turning darker, a heavy, angry dusk creeps slowly and icily through the little window, enveloping in black the damp walls, the low ceiling, the table with its white tablecloth, even Grandfather's white beard.

Dark.

And soon I hear Grandfather rise from his place, scrape together the challah crumbs from the late afternoon Sabbath meal, wrap a thick scarf around his neck, and leave.

With wide-open eyes and beating heart I stay where I am, enveloped in shadow. I listen: Everything around is silent. Only from further away, from the top of the hill, can a monotonous ringing be heard.

Clang-clang-clang! . . . clang-clang-clang!

The church bells are proclaiming that our holy Sabbath is passing away, and now it's their holy day, the uphill folk's.

Clang-clang-clang!

Slowly. Every peal distinct. And the wind rocks, rocks and sways:

"Ay-ay-ay . . . ay-ay-ay . . ."

That was exactly how my mother howled the night her two sons died on her.

But now a powerful ray of light suddenly pierces the little window, covers the table, scatters into many golden threads, and stabs my eyes: the old solid-walled synagogue, which towers over the hovels around its courtyard like a giant among midgets, watches me with seven fiery eyes—its lit windows. There, in the study hall, they're praying the evening service. The winter hats sway, the men spit out the closing prayer, wish each other "a good week."

Grandfather comes in, lights two thin candles, pours himself a little glass of Havdalah wine, and looks toward the door. Soon an ugly little kid walks in—he's the one who's going to be drinking that wine. He gives me a look with his small, devious eyes, waits for my grandfather to look away, and then sticks out his tongue. If it weren't for Grandfather, I'm sure that loathsome boy with his grubby paws would just stick his fist under my nose: "Here, take this."

I feel the blood rising to my head: You rotten snot-nose!

"Zeyde," I say, "Zeyde, I'll drink the wine today."

He shakes his head.

"Child, child—the Havdalah wine? You forget, you're a girl ..."

Child, child ... these words ring so bare, so strange. Two deep, deep creases spread across his high, pale brow, his milk-clouded eyes open wider and wider. Now all I can see are two gaping holes, they look off toward the corner between the window and partition.

"Beyla, Beyla, what did you do? You couldn't have borne me a kaddish, Beyla, huh ... ?"

And he stretches out a palsied hand, his right hand, the fingers long, pale, the nails sharp and cold.

"Beyla, oh Beyla."

And he bursts into tears. I can see his eyebrows trembling now, the tears rolling down.

"Zeyde ..." I lift my head.

Pacified-saddened now, he sits over the open Talmud, swaying and chanting softly.

He is learning—my soul fills to the brim with happiness. Suddenly, I remember that somewhere in one of the shacks at the very bottom of the hill lives an old Jewish woman, an ancient one. For five kopecks a week she'll teach anyone who asks how to read Hebrew.

"Five kopecks a week," I say to myself, and I feel a warm flow seep slowly into my heart and gently, silently caress it . . .

So one beautiful summer Sabbath I go over to Grandfather with tremulous steps and raise my two eyes—full of quiet, holy joy—to his.

"Want to test me, Zeyde?"

Grandfather lifts his head from the Talmud and brushes his brow with his hand. I see an eyelid tremble as he looks at me:

"Child."

"Zeyde," I blurt out, and feel as if my heart were about to burst in my chest. "Zeyde, test me."

He goes to the bookshelf, takes out a prayer book, opens it, and sets it before me. I lower my eyes and look into it.

Yisgadal veyiskadash shemey raba . . . the "Kaddish" . . . A sweet shudder runs through my entire body. I push the prayer book away with both hands, raise my head, and piously close my eyes.

"Yisgadal veyiskadash shemey raba."

And the words flow from my lips, they pour out of me into the air so mildly, so sadly . . . I feel my face flush, break out in a heavy sweat, my heart beats and beats and I keep reciting . . .

And suddenly, Grandfather snatches me in both arms, lifts me up on high, to the ceiling, and rising and soaring himself he carries the two of us floating through the house, rocking me and tossing me into the air and adorning me with psalms of praise:

"Holy Sabbath, holy Sabbath, holy Sabbath."

Purplish red are his lips, his high forehead—pure white. His long beard flies in all directions, quivering, and among the strands—two large teardrops shimmer and tremble now like a pair of diamonds.

Just a few days later I'm sitting on a big rock outside the synagogue wall with my head bowed—a congealed sorrow in my heart, two warm tears in my eyes. Over there, in our little house, a single memorial candle is burning, I can't forget that for a minute. Somewhere on the dirt floor a bundle of trampled straw has been strewn; scraps of white linen—remnants of Grandfather's shroud; on the door—a lock, a black, round lock . . . But what do I care? If only I had a black dress, an entirely black dress, I would look more like a boy, a lot more—this, it turns out, is the thought that's spinning in my brain.

Around me women are gathering, wagging their heads.

"So what do you suppose will happen to the orphan girl now?"

One of them even strokes my hair. "Would you like a little bun, maybe?"

A band of schoolboys shows up, looking at me with fascinated pity, and I announce to them very earnestly: "I'm not afraid of you."

I jump up from my place and follow them.

"Where are you going?" they ask.

"I'm going to the study hall," I say and at once feel both my knees start shaking. "I'm going to say kaddish."

"She's going to say kaddish," they snort, and an acrid, stuffy whiff of boy-sweat sears my nostrils. There are men all around me, blocking my way to the lectern, pushing me back—out—

out to the entry hall. But from above, from the Holy Ark, two thoughtful-pious eyes look down at me:

"Child, child ... ," so lonesome, so beseeching. "Child, child ... ," and only I see the light of the memorial candle by the lectern overflow into a burning ocean, engulfing me on all sides. My breath catches and sticks in my throat.

And when I open my eyes I find myself lying with my head against the hard rock in the synagogue yard and around me, like an angry stepmother, the dark, quiet night. There, on the door to our little house, hangs a round black lock. I haven't forgotten that, and a great fear grips my soul. I lower my face to the damp earth and burst into tears, first softly with dry eyes, and then louder and louder.

Somewhere high up under the synagogue eaves a bird awakens, flutters its wings, and listens with dread.

From the Yiddish

Bubbe Henya

Swaddled in a gray shawl, a wig perched on her head and a walking stick in her hand, that was how she used to go down to the gulch every morning. She would make her way with small quiet steps. Whenever she passed anyone, she would take the time to greet them with a smile, to brighten their day.

"Good morning to you and to all good people everywhere!"

If she encountered a band of schoolboys, she always stopped to pass out filberts to some, almonds to others:

"Eat, children, so you'll have strength to study the holy Torah."

If she saw someone who was in pain, she would stroke them with her sad, moist eyes:

"I have just the herb for you, it will cure what ails you, make the pain disappear."

She had a voice, Bubbe Henya, a soft voice that always rang with sympathy.

The women of the gulch would greet her with beaming faces:

"I have a whole pot of leftover cream soup, Bubbe. I tucked it away for your poor folk."

"I saved up three bagels for you. Open your apron, Bubbe, dear."

Bubbe Henya would nod:

"For that mitzvah, you won't end up depending on the kindness of strangers."

And with short, sprightly steps she would continue on her way.

They would follow her down the street with long, reverent gazes:

"They say that she takes from her own pocket even more than she collects from others."

"But where does she get it? What does she survive on?"

The neighbor women explain:

Night after night, when the last fire in the gulch houses has been extinguished and the lamp blown out, she wakes up, opens her little book of Psalms and starts praising the Creator, may His name be a blessing. Next to the table she has a sack of feathers, and she takes a fistful and plucks the down from the quill, and takes another fistful and plucks some more. From the money she earns from this, she takes what she needs for herself, and she takes a share to distribute in the poorhouse, and she also puts a little aside toward the redemption of her soul.

For a long while, the gulch folk would whisper and shake their heads:

"What a woman."

And much later in the night, when a mute darkness surrounds the gulch houses, quick, sure footsteps would break the silence of the town. Those were Bubbe Henya's steps. Her wig disheveled, her shawl slipping down one shoulder, she would emerge from the poorhouse. Her thin hands would be clutching two small bodies close to her breast. Caressing them in the stillness, she would whisper a warm secret in each of their ears.

They were two little orphans, sick and abandoned after their mother had died. Bubbe Henya took them in, to recite Psalms over their little heads in the night, to wash them with her tears in the daytime. After they had recuperated but their legs were still weak, she would carry them to school every morning, hugging them close to her breast, so they could learn God's Torah. In the evening she would bring them back home. Her feet sure, her legs quick, in those days she didn't yet need a cane.

And this, now, is what the gulch women say about Bubbe Henya's arrival in town:

It happened once on a quiet and peaceful summer evening. The day had been a hot one. Everyone was sitting on their front steps, half-naked, talking and chattering away. Suddenly a commotion was heard, and down the hill, with a huge clanging, rolled a large carriage, followed by a column of dust, and inside that column, it turned out, an old woman was walking.

"Is there anyplace around here where I can spend the night?"

An hour later, she could be seen walking around town, moving from house to house.

"Are you looking for something, Bubbe?"

She shook her head happily.

"That's right, call me Bubbe. That suits me just fine."

And her eyes slid over the children's pale faces and snatched glimpses of the corners of the dilapidated little houses around.

People stared after her, unsettled and suspicious.

Who was she? Where had she come from? Had anyone asked her to come here?

But by the next morning, even before the sun had appeared at the top of the hill, everybody knew that, on that very night, they had been brushed by a hand bearing blessings from afar.

Children who had been sick energetically ran around the street, their cheeks a healthy, rosy color, their eyes shining; on their thin wrists, now, were tied red threads as talismans. Frail old people discovered bottles of an elixir on their doorsteps, which they drank, and felt their youthful vigor restored. And in the poorhouse alley, there was a feast on every table, on each and every table.

Soon after that, the following story made the rounds in the shtetl:

Her name was Henya. She came from the big city. There she had been a real lady, played an important role in community affairs. But tragedy struck: On the very day her first child was born, her husband passed away. She bathed that boy in her tears, she wrapped him in her own hair and she loved him enough for two. But once, when she was lying in bed with the child, taking too much pleasure in him, a death sentence descended upon her from the heavens. And her husband arose from his grave, appeared before her and pleaded:

"Wake up, rouse yourself from sleep and take a look at what you're doing to our child: You're suffocating him with your own two hands . . ." She heard every word he said, but somehow she couldn't move a muscle. And when she awoke the next morning and found, lying beside her, a bloody little corpse, she opened her prayer book, recited "Blessed is the Righteous Judge," and then lifted her arms toward heaven and said:

"The Lord giveth and the Lord taketh away."

After the week of mourning, she disposed of her property, distributing it among the poor, took up a walking stick—and arrived here in our shtetl.

Others told it differently:

The truth is she came from a nearby shtetl. There she had a husband and seven sons—all of them renowned, all of them sitting day and night over the Talmud. And she herself—she took in laundry, shelled chickpeas, and supported her family. And late, late in the night, when she had finished her work, she—as worn out and exhausted as she was—she would steal into the women's gallery of the synagogue, rest her head against the lattice, and listen. Eight voices, eight melodious and clear voices would flow together in one sad chant, filling the study hall with supernal light and floating up, up . . . At the eastern wall burned the lamp, illuminating the velvet curtain covering the Ark and the eight faces of her husband and children. She would take it all in and brim with pride and joy:

"Yes, that's my man . . . yes, these are my babies."

But the One above did not, as it were, care for these proud words and a fire descended from heaven and engulfed the holy house while all eight souls were between its high walls. The next morning, the wife and mother picked their scorched bones from the ashes with her bare hands. And when she returned home from the graveyard, she looked at the house and it was empty. From the bookshelves, entire rows of holy books looked out at her in speechless shame and, in a corner, she saw eight pairs of desolate phylacteries in a neat pile—so she tore her clothes in mourning, took off her shoes, sat on the ground, and raised both hands to God:

"You are just and your judgment is just."

Not a single tear did she shed, but her face became covered with deep wrinkles all over.

And when she arose from the seven days of mourning, she donated her house for Torah study and swore a solemn oath that she would devote her life to charity. Since then, there was no decree from God, blessed be He, so harsh that Bubbe Henya could not annul it with her tears . . .

That same evening the gulch folk added another prayer to their nighttime Shema:

"May it be God's will that the providence of this woman here shall never be removed from our midst."

Old people, on that same night, saw in their dreams:

Entire bands of angels, all of them pure, all of them radiant, spread their wings over the squat shacks of the gulch, floating above them and protecting them.

And in the gulch, the women told yet another story:

The shtetl had about a dozen or so orphan girls. Some of these girls' braids were already turning gray and they were starting to lose their teeth, others were getting wrinkled and withered, and every single one of them was gnawed by hunger and wretchedly poor. Bubbe Henya put together a few coins, one penny at a time, to sew them wedding dresses, she looked high and low for nice boys for them to marry, and then married them off one by one. It so happened that the last of these orphan girls had moved to a village and the wedding was held there, so Henya was gone from the gulch for two days. But before the first day had passed, awful news rattled every heart.

A mother of six small children was having terrible labor pains, the midwife wasn't holding out much hope, and where was Bubbe Henya now?

In the gulch, chaos reigned. Young wives carried boiling water from the bathhouse, filling basins, old women wrung their hands and argued with God, blessed be He . . . Relatives banged their heads against the wall, wailing loudly. In the synagogue, ten old men gathered to rend the heavens with their Psalms.

Toward evening the laboring woman recited her deathbed confession and took leave of her children. That was when the people of the gulch declared with one voice:

"We've got to bring Bubbe Henya back."

With quiet steps, with small steps she came back to town. Deep sorrow shrouded her wan face. Her good, moist eyes looked off, over there, toward the graveyard. And that, in fact, was where she headed.

As they saw her coming back down the hill, with a confident step, her face shining with joy, people's hearts beat happily and they breathed ever so easily, ever so calmly:

"When Bubbe Henya puts her mind to something, it gets done."

When the gulch folk gathered on the eighth day for the circumcision, the baby's mother served the guests herself . . . That Bubbe Henya was destined to live out her full allotment of seventy years was clear as day to them all. But she was torn from this world in the sixty-fifth year of her life, and this, now, is how it happened:

One fine summer day, a black cloud loomed over the gulch folk: Their rabbi had laid himself down with no warning, become paralyzed and lost the power of speech, the doctor from up the hill had given up hope for his recovery.

The whole community, shaken to the core, gathered in the synagogue. A fast day was decreed, psalms were recited, loud sobs rose from the women's section, even the little children prayed their hearts out—but to no avail; in the midst of it all, the rabbi's wife stormed into the synagogue. Her face was as white as a sheet, she was screaming to high heavens:

"Friends, we are losing the crown of our shtetl. He already sees the grim old man wrapped in black before his very eyes."

When the crowd turned toward the door, they found their way blocked by a gaunt body:

"Where are you going?"

It was Bubbe Henya.

Her two radiant eyes—two seas of compassion—looked first at one of them, then at another:

"Friends, seventy are the years of a person's life. I am sixty-five—the rest I give to our rabbi—let anyone whose heart is so moved give a share too . . ."

And two days later, Bubbe Henya was going from house to house, saying:

"I'm donating a Torah scroll to the old synagogue—come celebrate with me."

By now she was walking with two canes.

And when the sun set and evening came, tens of thousands of little flames flickered in the air. It was the gulch folk, lighting the way for Bubbe Henya's canopy with candles and torches, lanterns and lamps. Klezmer musicians with long trumpets led the way for her, women adorned in satin and silk and the elderly rabbi surrounded by dignified old men walked behind her, and Bubbe Henya floated along under the wedding canopy with her Torah, the holy scroll pressed to her heart, two glistening tears in her eyes.

And when they placed the Torah scroll beside its sisters and closed the Holy Ark and covered it with its velvet curtain, Bubbe Henya jumped up to the pulpit, flung aside her two canes, and stretched her arms heavenward.

Suddenly she stood tall, her face became youthful, and her eyes—two black suns.

"Ay, ay, Father in Heaven ... Ay, ay, Master of the Universe! ..."

With quick and sure steps she circled the pulpit, walked out of the synagogue, and turned toward the poorhouse:

"Ay, ay, Father in Heaven ... Ay, ay, Master of the Universe! ..."

And now, hands linked together and a great circle formed, a beautiful circle, the klezmorim blew their trumpets, old folk snapped their fingers, women clapped their hands, and they surged and streamed closer and closer to the poorhouse. Ten thousand flames flickered in the still air. Far away, in the distant east, a pale morning star stared with amazement at the gulch.

The next night, the gulch folk made their way home from the graveyard, their faces white as shrouds. Every once in a while a sigh would escape one of them, quiver for a moment, and then fade away. A great darkness reigned, and each of them walked down that mountain alone, groping for solid ground beneath their feet . . .

From the mountain glowed the enormous church, threatening them all with its uncanny pallor. Down in the gulch, the dogs howled.

From the Yiddish

An Only Daughter

Early one fine morning, the mumbling of voices from Mama's bedroom startles me awake. In the dining room, someone is speaking in a hoarse voice and coughing.

Is that Bubbe? She came all the way here from three streets over—so early!

Amazed and unsettled, my gaze wanders restlessly around the room before it fixes itself, in stunned horror, on the small table: No milk, no buns! Is Mama planning on letting me die of starvation?

"Mariashka!"

But instead of the maid, some burly Jewish woman with her sleeves rolled up pushes through the door.

"Hey you, settle down, stop that screeching," and with cold, glassy eyes she looks me over and then she disappears.

In the dining room, beside the simmering samovar, sits Papa. Stroking his thick black beard, he gazes at me with a smile: "So, Rochele! . . ."

And then I see my grandmother. Standing at the eastern wall, an open prayer book in hand, she rapidly leafs through the pages, gesturing to me without interrupting her prayers, "Nu, oh . . . ," and she shrewdly, slyly winks toward my mother's room: "Oy, nu . . ."

It's the maid who finally lets out the secret. Having helped the burly Jewish woman carry a large basin of water from Mama's room, she closes the bedroom door quickly and sticks out a long tongue.

"Nyah, nyah, nyah! For eight years the only one and now— it's all over!"

"Huh?"

Before my eyes I can see—like an open grave—my grandmother's toothless mouth: "Ha, ha, ha, take a look . . . look at that girl's face turning colors . . . ha, ha, ha."

A little while later, Grandmother relaxes in an armchair and she and my father put their heads together: "So, what do you say, maybe her name really should be 'Masha'? That would be in honor of Aunt Matl, of blessed memory."

And she adds: "May you only live to lead her to the wedding canopy, God willing."

And she squints her red-rimmed eyes so comically that for the first time in my life I notice an extra, swollen fold of skin dangling from her throat, quivering strangely whenever she speaks. I couldn't control myself.

"Hey, Bubbe. What's that disgusting thing on your neck?" I titter.

And then something happens that has never happened to me before: Papa, his face bright red and his eyes bulging, storms over to me: "What did you say? Huh? What was that?"

That was how our neighbor Barukh was always looking at my friend Feygele, who had five sisters younger than her.

My heart pounds. Suddenly I feel as if all the people in the room had somehow become strangers to me, conspiring against me. Even him, I think, looking at my father, and a cold hatred blossoms in my heart for that hairy man.

I'm going to run away from them all, I decide on the spur of the moment and make for the door. I won't come home for three whole days and nights. I'll sleep in the abandoned house at the end of the street. And food? I'll smuggle a piece of bread out with me.

In the hall, Mariashka meets me with a glass of coffee.

"Come on, you have to eat something, your Mama said so."

"Go tell her that I won't eat, and make sure she hears it," I hurl at her face.

In the corner, under the staircase, I spot Tzuly, my kitten, eyes half-closed, lying stretched out, breathing peacefully. I take it all out on her. "No, no, no, you should know better than that . . ." I tear at her ears, drag her from the corner by the tail and start plucking out her fur, one hair at a time.

A few days later Mariashka approaches me, taking me by the hand.

"Come, Mama's calling you."

The blood rushes to my face.

"Mama?"

In fact, I've been anticipating this moment for a long time. Many times before this, I had sneaked up to her door, stood there with my heart pounding, and listened. More than once, it has occurred to me that the whole thing was a lie, that there was nothing going on in that room, they were just hiding her from me to tease me . . . But now they were calling me to Mama. Soon I would see her, hug her, tell her everything, everything, and again she would stroke me with her good eyes.

"Now, listen when they tell you to do something, my one and only . . ."

The door opens quietly . . . Mama—her face so pale, drawn, and the eyes smile so strangely.

"Want to see?"

My knees buckle.

Is it true, then? Yes, yes, now I see my own brown cradle. From inside of it I can hear soft breathing.

"Want a look?" And she snatches some wrapped-up thing from the cradle: a little red face, a wide mouth, and two tiny green eyes.

"Smoo-oooch . . ." Mama gives the thing a kiss. She pulls it to her heart: "My daughter."

"MAMA!"

And I want to throw myself at her feet, sobbing and howling: "What are you doing? STOP!"

She suddenly takes my hand and passes it over the tiny face, which is damp, soft, so very warm.

"Hold your little sister, go on, hold her."

B-r-r-r . . . a cold sweat breaks out over my entire body, I snatch my hand away and blurt out: "I wish it would die."

And frightened by my own words, I run from the room:

My head is dizzy and the world spins before my eyes. I suddenly remember that once there was just such a little red-faced creature at a neighbor's house, and its own mother rolled over on it in her sleep. The next morning they took it out of the room and never brought it back again.

A strange idea runs through my head like a lightning bolt.

I'm sitting in my room with a pale face and a heavy head, looking restlessly at the clock. Half past four . . . a quarter to five . . . just a little longer. My heart beats heavy and slow: the time has finally come which I've so impatiently awaited—Yom Kippur eve. Tonight my mother will be away all evening. Papa will also be in the synagogue, Mariashka will be in the kitchen, and I'll be with *her*—in the bedroom . . . It will be dark everywhere; I'll go over quietly, I'll lay myself down . . . wait a while—and then . . . "Rochele!" Dressed in white silk, a yellow embroidered kerchief on her head, Mama comes in, pale, her eyes moist and good.

"A happy new year to you, my daughter!"

So delicate and so warm! It's just the way it was in the good old days, when I was hers alone. A sweet shudder runs through me, my heart beats faster:

Should I tell her, should I spill it all?

"Don't leave me here tonight, don't go, Mama . . ."

"But it's Yom Kippur eve, my child!" And then: "I'm not so worried about you, but I hate to leave little Masha . . . Oh!"

"What was that, Mama?"

Mama's dress had rustled. It was Papa, in his white Yom Kippur caftan, closing the door behind him.

Ticktock, ticktock! Was that the clock on the wall or was it the heart in my chest?

Quietly, in the distance, a soft singing starts up. A thick darkness huddles against the window. A thin, smoking memorial candle burns quietly, pensively. On the wall, my shadow quivers for a while, suddenly stretches itself out along the floor, and then follows me to the bedroom:

"Mariashka?"

And between my hands I can feel a trembling, soft, damp body.

"Ugh." A strangled voice. Two glinting eyes.

I can hear brisk footsteps from the dining room. Hundreds of sparks swim before my eyes. The flame of the memorial candle overflows into a fiery sea.

To this very day, when the end of Yom Kippur arrives every year and Mama in her white silk dress sits down at the table to break her fast, she suddenly recollects: "Do you remember, Motl, how once on Yom Kippur we found our Rochele in a faint, her kitten Tzuly lying near her, suffocated?"

My sister Masha—she's grown up by now, twelve years old, with two thick braids and dimples in both cheeks (oh, how I hate those dimples)—listens, opens her mouth wide, and laughs. Her small green eyes glint so strangely and her face turns so red that I'm sure if I were to touch it now it would feel warm, soft, and damp, and a weird shudder travels through me.

From the Yiddish

Fedka

At sunrise, when all the shtetl folk are still indoors, sound asleep—Fedka hurries out onto the steps of the post office and faces east. A long and narrow paved road stretches before him, squeezed between two expansive fields; Fedka squints his large, penetrating eyes, balls his fist into a kind of cylinder, raises it, and peers through for a long time. He makes out a wavering black dot, steadily approaching town—the postal carriage is returning from the train station—and he moves now, folds his hands behind his back, and starts pacing the length of the landing. He's a giant of a man, he holds that back of his very straight and his head is always held so high. That tight little jacket of his—it's a postman's jacket, all spruced up with two rows of close-set, shiny buttons—makes him utterly charming to look at. His swarthy face is freshly scrubbed, his shock of hair is wet, glossy black, and a little tousled. A few stray cowlicks stand erect, and another two or three curls tumble over his forehead, tickling his brow. These curls bounce a little now as he walks,

half-scratching, half-caressing him. Fedka shoots a glance upward to get a look at those curls and smiles.

In the meantime, the shtetl has begun to stir. A cock crows,
and the sound travels from one end of the shtetl to the other.
Gates creak open and a few cows lumber out of the dark cow-
sheds and step into the street one at a time, chewing their cud
lazily. They raise their heads, flick their tails, and let out a
truncated moo with every blast of their cowherd's horn. Some
woman, bare feet tucked into wooden clogs, pumps the water
hoist with all her might, filling the bucket, which is covered
with some sort of dripping slime, and then emptying the water
into her own jugs. The water splashes loudly, a few drops spray-
ing out to the sides and glistening in the rising sun like tiny
sapphires. The town billy goat stands before a fence, hugging
a pole with his two front hooves, peels off a few strips of bark,
and chews them. Shutters swing open, smoke begins to rise
from the chimneys, wheels clatter on the cobblestones: the
postal carriage is pulling up to the post office; Fedka reaches
the carriage in a single bound, pounces on the big leather sack,
lifts it with one hand, and pulls it close to his chest. His other
hand is moving over and sifting the contents of the sack, making the paper envelopes and postcards rustle. Fedka's heart
pounds:

If only he knew whose day he was going to make today and
whom he was going to disappoint!

And this thought—which is directed entirely toward the
hundred Jewish families that live there, in the gulch, who are
all just either little children, or dried-up old people, or young
girls or women whose husbands had wandered off abroad . . .

The clock chimes nine. Fedka picks up his leather satchel,

hoists the strap over his shoulder, and pulling it in a taut diagonal across his chest, clutches the satchel under his arm and makes his way toward town.

He passes through the street where his own people live—the gentile street—very quickly. He only slows down here for a moment beside the doctor's house to hand over a rolled-up magazine, and then he turns away and lengthens his stride. The doctor's housekeeper, a fat, jovial peasant woman, follows him with a long, lustful gaze. Flaxen and golden heads can be seen through the open windows—the girls of the street are watching him. A few of them even blow him a kiss. Fedka—he doesn't favor them with even a single glance. He just keeps walking with his firm, steady, rough step, striking his stick every once in a while on the cobblestones and leaving a thin column of dust in his wake, which dissipates behind him. He's pulled himself up to his full, impressive height. His right arm embraces the leather bag, stuffed with sealed and unsealed letters and postcards, and he hugs it close to his chest.

But when he arrives at the bottom of the sloping street and the gulch opens up before him, his step becomes lighter and his eyes are touched with a smile. From most of the porches and through the windows and over each threshold, eyes stare out at Fedka, looking him over with an expression that's both hopeful and afraid. Women jump off the stoops, take the stairs two or three at a time, and head in his direction. Young girls throw down their work, pull their rolled-up sleeves down, and turning to look at Fedka with flushed faces and eager smiles, they hurry toward him too, the hems of their dresses fluttering as they run. Barefoot young children pop out of every doorway of the street, pulling their rumpled caps off as they run to greet the postman. And he, well he's walking at a leisurely pace now, slipping himself into the gang of women and children that's growing larger by the minute, his lazy gaze resting first on one face and then on another. His hand is already in the satchel, riffling through the letters, fingering them, crumpling them . . . he sees that all eyes are now on this hand, with restless anticipation, but he deliberately leaves his hand in the satchel for a moment longer. He couldn't be standing more erect, towering head and shoulders above the crowd, his agile body all in black standing out against the women's worn-out dresses, his cap pushed back and his shock of black hair gleaming in the sun. Feeling at the height of his power and good looks now, Fedka whistles a Jewish tune and smiles:

"The truth is that the only reason I came here is to let you know that your people are finally getting down to writing a letter."

He speaks a broken Yiddish, rolling his *r* and sounding the *h* like a *kh*. The people around him laugh, shaking their fingers at him, threatening and pleading with him:

"Okay, wise guy, smart aleck, how long are you planning on teasing us?"

Fedka laughs too, taking a large envelope from his satchel and waving it in the air, his eyes moving searchingly through the band.

"Hey, where's that little fatso Pesl? Looks like your guy is sending you his mug shot."

The young woman breaks into a heavy sweat, her face rapidly turning a succession of shades; she stretches all ten fingers toward the envelope, the group closing in now and squeezing into a tighter circle. Old women arm themselves with their spectacles and crane their necks, even the little ones push themselves in among the adults, standing on tiptoe, the whole crowd waiting curiously.

Fedka rips the envelope open himself. Slowly he exposes the photograph within it, gives it a look and laughs:

"No beard, no sidelocks, I swear by my Jewish soul, he looks just like the pharmacist."

And again he puts his hand into the satchel:

"Brayne, is she here? Your husband's sent you a check for thirty rubles . . ."

Sometimes a woman would suddenly elbow her way into the crowd, panting with exertion, her face flushed and perspiring, clutching something in her hand:

"Fedka, brother, have pity, it got stuck and—I can't do a thing with it . . . Everybody in the gulch has already tried," she says, holding out a large bottle toward him.

Fedka tosses his satchel and stick on the ground, takes the bottle, gives it a twist and a turn, and yanks out the shiny glass stopper:

"Ay, women, women, women."

The women murmur respectfully:

"Ah! Those are the hands of a man . . ."

"A real man . . ."

Fedka hears the praise and falls silent, he quickly empties his satchel of the rest of the letters, picks up his stick, and moves off toward the hill, toward home.

Feeling the eyes of the gulch folk caressing his back and sensing them whisper his name—he straightens himself up to his full height.

Sometimes a dark summer night would suddenly be utterly illuminated: the Jewish street was on fire. There were no fire-fighters in town. The fire, like a slave girl set free, would hurl flames in every direction, sticking out her long red tongue, licking at the nearby roofs, her uncanny hunger threatening to swallow more and more houses; then beams would fall with a crash, girders heave and collapse. Now a wall buckles and dis-integrates in all directions, then a roof is struck and drops to the ground, scattering sparks everywhere. Chaos in the gulch. Frightened cows, released from their sheds, wander around in clusters, huddling against each other and lowing. Roosters with feathers askew scurry in blind circles, their eyes wide open, pecking and letting out earsplitting crows. Dogs bark and howl. From the top of the hill the church bells toll mournfully. Bare-foot half-naked women raise their hands to the crimson sky, hurling complaints against their fortune. Shivering babies drag along behind, scratching and wailing loudly. And as the uphill folk gather up their belongings and rush off to the other part of the shtetl to save their skins, Fedka slips out of the post office, grabs a few buckets and some rope, and makes tracks to the Jewish street. From afar, he waves his arms to try to quiet the screeches and wails. His mind is crystal clear, he's fearless in the face of peril, he chooses a house at the very center of the inferno, enters it, shoulders a load of pillows and quilts, and carries them over to the meadow. Women surround him on all sides, stretching their palms toward him, blessing and pleading with him at the same time, and Fedka calms them each down.

"Don't worry so much, you silly things—don't you see that I'm right here with you? . . ."

And when a pale dawn breaks and rises after a night like that, the fire has already died down. From the ruins a column of smoke twists up, mingling with the stench of scorched hides and melted tallow. Singed belongings and broken furniture are piled in heaps in the meadow. Babies lie sunk in slumber atop sooty pillows and featherbeds, and Fedka is here, too. His shock of hair is disheveled, his face covered with a layer of sweat, he brushes his clothes off with a rag and talks with the band of women around him; they give him warm looks:

"How can we ever repay you for everything you've done, Fedka—maybe on your wedding day?"

And Fedka jokes:

"How can I ever get married when I have my hands full taking care of dozens of women!"

And he gestures at the circle. They all laugh, shaking their heads:

"Nu, think about it, Fedka. Ach, if it weren't for you—what could we have done on a night like this? A flock of women . . ."

Fedka pretends he hasn't heard. He picks out a path among the heaps of possessions strewn across the meadow and heads toward the post office.

"And now I'm off to bring you good tidings from abroad."

On Sabbaths, he delivers the mail a little later. He waits to go down to the gulch until he knows that lunch is being served there. The Jewish street is quiet at this hour. The Sabbath sun rests its rays here, pouring powerful light and warmth into every nook and cranny. Goats stroll lazily around, looking off into space and dreaming. The smell of noodle kugel and turnips suffuses the air. Fedka breathes in the aroma with enormous pleasure and, as he strides with quiet steps, he listens to the clatter of forks and spoons that bursts through the open windows. As he walks he takes a letter out of his satchel, opens it, and walks into some house:

"Good Shabbes!"

He's always greeted affectionately. The woman of the house fills a plate with kugel, sets it before Fedka, and urges him on:

"It's getting cold!"

Fedka lifts a spoonful of kugel to his lips and makes the blessing:

"Blessed arrrt thou, etc., etc. who brings forth brrrrread from the earrrrth."

Laughing, the woman of the house pats him on the shoulder:

"Nu, would you believe, Fedka, that sometimes I think: If only our Fedka was a Jew—if only—I wonder how many women's obligation to hear kiddush he would fulfill with just one blessing over the wine."

Fedka takes his satchel off and sets it down beside him. They chat about gulch matters, of family affairs. The woman of the house boasts about her children's accomplishments or lists her complaints:

"This one here, at the end of the table, he's shooting up from one day to the next," and she asks, "but what's he going to do with himself?"

Fedka looks at the boy in question, and his face suddenly grows solemn:

"It's true, he really is becoming quite a man . . . I hadn't noticed it before."

And he takes the boy's measure with an unsettled expression that is out of character for him.

"Those shoulders . . . and there are signs of a beard, if I'm not mistaken . . ."

And a second later he tosses off:

"And the gulch women aren't flirting with him yet?"

He's joking, but a whimsical glint flashes and trembles in his eyes.

"If you want my advice—I'd ship him off to America, ship him right off."

And he doesn't let up until he sees that his admonition has been taken to heart.

And it goes on this way until he leaves to deliver a letter to another house, where they're already preparing for the afternoon nap. The shutters are closed, the house is stifling and dark. Women and girls dressed in short nightgowns and slips try to scurry away from Fedka in their embarrassment, but Fedka hushes them, waving his arms:

"Sh-sh-sh-sh-sh . . ."

As if absentmindedly his hand grazes a soft, heaving breast; on his face he suddenly feels a panting breath that makes his blood sizzle:

"Fed-ka-a-a . . ."

And by the time he leaves the gulch the sun is already low on the western horizon. In the churches the bells are chiming to announce the imminent arrival of Sunday—the Christian day of rest. From afar Fedka sees many of the people who live on his street, dressed in their Sunday finest, streaming toward church. Fedka pays them no heed. His heart brims over now with restful sensations, with infinite Sabbath joy. He passes between two rows of squat houses, the last of the gulch homes, at a leisurely pace. Women are sitting in small bunches on their front steps and chatting. They're talking about him, about Fedka. Nobody knows where he's from, who he is, what he is. There are some who even doubt that he's a Christian:

"The man, he must have been a Jew. If he converted, it was only so that he'd be allowed to tear open envelopes on Sabbath."

Others protest:

"Fedka was never a Jew in his life, but what it is, he worked for a long time in rich Jewish houses. Once he was in terrible danger and the Jews he worked for saved him, and he swore from then on to be good to Jews."

And they assure everyone:

"From the day he took the position as postman in the shtetl, no bad news from abroad ever came through the mail."

Fedka senses them talking about him. He can feel the women's eyes on his back, sometimes he even catches his name on some woman's lips. He walks along gracefully, striking his stick on the cobblestones and smiling. Unawares, he hums a well-known Jewish tune.

He has a pure and clear voice, Fedka does.

But it would often happen that Fedka would suddenly become sad, his face would grow old and cloud over. And this would happen, of all things, just when the gulch residents were feeling particularly happy: Two or three "Americans" have returned home for a holiday. The whole gulch rings with joy. Women spruce themselves up, put on their old wedding dresses, rouge their cheeks, and with clanging necklaces and bracelets (sent from America), they go over to the houses where the guests are staying, greeting the women of the house:

"I hope you're enjoying your guests!"

"If only you enjoyed your whole life as much as I'm enjoying myself now."

The house is full. Children bring in bottles of wine to serve the new arrivals. Nuts are cracked, glasses clink. The guests deliver regards to the women of the gulch from their menfolk.

On a Sabbath like this one, the postal sack lies ashamed and abandoned on the carriage floor. Fedka—his heart had told him what was in store, and he hasn't even gone out to the landing to meet the carriage. He goes down to the gulch even later than he usually does on Sabbaths. From a distance he can already see the women of the street, crowding on the guests' porches. Their colorful dresses shine in the sun, watch chains and earrings dazzle the eye, and among these women's dresses stand out black coattails, top hats, clean-shaven faces—young men.

His heart is cut to the quick. He hurries to pass out the two or three postcards in his satchel and turns away. Women block his path, trying to stop him:

"Come listen to what they're saying about my Henich . . . Why shouldn't you share a little in my joy."

Young girls grab the lapels of his jacket:

"No, this time you're not getting away, the time has come for you to have fun when we do."

He stands silent.

They look at him quizzically:

"Fedka, what's wrong? Does something hurt? Are you feeling well?"

"Leave me alone."

And his head hanging, he stomps away from the gulch.

Toward evening, as the church bell chimes steadily, a thick

column of dust appears on the post-office street: the residents of the gulch are out for a stroll. The guests, with their wives and children beside them, walk at the head, and after them follow a throng of women and girls, two or three bent-over, dried-out old men, bounding children.

On one of the benches on the post-office landing sits the postmaster, across from him his wife and Fedka. The postmaster gives the strolling band a long look and mutters:

"They say those people brought piles of money from America."

Fedka flares up:

"Nobody actually counted it, they just say, right?"

The postmaster's wife muses:

"Money—what can people like that do with money? The last ruble runs out and then what?"

Fedka shoots her a grateful look, presses both hands over his heart, and adds:

"Those eels! If some war broke out right now in Russia, they'd slip away in a hot minute."

And a muffled curse escapes from his lips and chases after the gulch folk, who by now have moved further and further away from town.

Aggravation

At the home of the businessman Shlomo Aaronson the following events transpired:

Once, on a cold and overcast autumn day at four o'clock in the afternoon, his bookkeeper, Levi Levine, entered the dining room, paused at the threshold, and said that he, Levi Levine, had come to ask for a certain sum of rubles as an advance on next month's salary, since he urgently needed this certain sum of rubles, in fact it was a terrible emergency, otherwise—he said—he wouldn't dream of asking.

This happened at four o'clock in the afternoon, which is why the pleasant scent of lemon and various desserts, of oranges and apples, now suffused Mr. Shlomo Aaronson's dining room, and on the table stood full steaming cups and a polished hissing samovar and small saucers of preserves at each and every setting.

Aside from these objects, present in the room were also Mrs. Aaronson herself, and Matya and Petya, her children, and the governess, the children's governess, who sat at the black piano picking out a tune with slender, very white fingers—and Mr. Aaronson was pacing back and forth on the soft carpets, enjoying a fragrant cigarette for his own pleasure and his household's enjoyment too.

This Shlomo Aaronson was a stout, hulking man, his body strong and very erect, and his steps as he paced were assertive and confident, and the watch chain across his chest rattled and glittered, and his eyes, armed with gold spectacles, radiated power and arrogance.

Of a different breed was Levi Levine, who stood at the threshold and laid out his plea in the matter of a certain sum of rubles; he wasn't the sort to stride with any confidence, and he was short and had no high opinion of himself, and when all was said and done he was just another hard-up fellow, a poor young man who spent his days squinting at tiny numerals in oversized account ledgers, and he was just as skinny and mute and solitary as one of those numerals.

And here it should be noted that there was no call at all for an insignificant office worker to come to the house of his employer and create a ruckus with trivial requests, just when the members of the household had assembled in anticipation of a pleasant repast. For circumstances like these there was, after all, an office in the warehouse and hours set aside for such purposes and so on. And there's no need to add that any extra verbiage as to a desperate situation, poverty, hunger, et al., were utterly and maddeningly superfluous, when the man of the house was explaining to you with perfect brevity that he never gave an advance to anyone, on principle he never gave advances.

It was no wonder, then, that this entire negotiation grated

on the nerves of everyone in the house and left an irritable mood in its wake.

In a short while, however, the impression left by this episode had dissipated, thanks to the ringing of the doorbell and the voices of guests coming in through the foyer.

This was the hour for tea and fruit in every more or less respectable home, and Mrs. Aaronson, rising to greet her guests, ordered the maids to bring in a few more cups and teaspoons and some more oranges and apples. The man of the house then opened a pack of cigarettes and offered cigarettes to the men, and chocolate to the women, and the conversation—about the weather, about the incredibly muddy streets of the city, which were muddier than anyone remembered them—began.

As concerns the bookkeeper Levi Levine, he now had to find, in the foyer, his hat and coat (it was the one coat mud-stained from those streets!), a task whose difficulty was rather aggravated by the other coats that hung there in a jumble, the coats of the other visitors. Moreover, he was now accosted by Petya, his employer's younger son, who tried to strike up a conversation with him.

He, the bookkeeper, evaded these attempts, though, saying that he had to hurry away immediately since there, downstairs, in the office, he had left the account ledgers lying open and out of order; but Petya, the employer's son, mocked him and responded that that was a lie, a damned lie, and the only reason he was trying to rush off was because he was shy and stupid— stupid, stupid, stupid—the boy slapped him on the back, jumped up, and stuck out his tongue at him. And for a long time the bookkeeper struggled in the gloom between the door and coatrack, fumbling among the hooks above—in search of his coat.

All this took place, as mentioned above, on an overcast autumn day, at four o'clock in the afternoon; and by approximately eight or eight-thirty the next morning, just as Mr. Aaronson was emerging from his bedroom in dressing gown and slippers—a new development ensued. From the bottom floor, from the warehouse, came one of the floor clerks, removed his cap, and informed the boss that below, in the office, something untoward had happened, that the bookkeeper Levi Levine (who knows how he had managed to spend the night there?) had taken his own life beside the desk and the account ledgers, the open account ledgers. The manager, who was in charge of all business matters, had yet to arrive, and the floor clerks were at a loss—should the police be notified?

All this the boy transmitted in a stammer, in fits and starts, but with his voice reserved and half-audible, as befits a worker standing before his employer. Nevertheless Mrs. Aaronson, whose bedroom door was ajar, heard the story from beginning to end, and without a thought to her unkempt hair and her disheveled, sleep-rumpled appearance, leaped out of bed, threw something on, and hurried to the parlor, to the clerk and her husband. Since—first of all it was crucial to hush the two of them and kick them for heaven's sake out of that room; the children, Petya and Matya, hadn't gone off to school yet, and may God save them, the little things, from such news. And second of all? Second of all—Oh heavens, my dear heavens—she went into the dining room and began to pace back and forth, now stopping at one window and now at the other window: "No. Solomon, you come here right now, and look, just look at those salespeople from the little shops, look at them milling around, they're going into our warehouse and the policemen, look, look at those lowlifes, they can't get enough of the sight . . ."

At that moment the skies hung dark and low, and the fog was dense in all directions, and the wind was blowing, and rain fell—a cold, penetrating rain, and the neighbors on the street below, longtime friends and acquaintances of Shlomo Aaronson, after they had lingered outside the warehouse for a bit, came over and rang the doorbell and ascended to the upper floor, drenched in rain and damp and mutual sorrow.

Now, with the mood in the house gloomy and every face dejected, no one stood on ceremony; they entered the dining room without unnecessary bows or curtsies, raised questions and poured themselves tea without waiting for an invitation from the hostess or anyone to serve them; and even though the silver tongs lay polished and ready on the table as always, everyone stuck their hands into the sugar bowl, scrabbled around among the sugar cubes for one that was the right size, and crumbled the biscuits with their fingers and nails.

That the managing director of the business was a scoundrel, on that there was now unanimous consent; after all, he was the one who was in charge, and he was paid a handsome salary for it, too, and he was the one responsible for keeping order. Because, after all, the warehouse shouldn't be allowed to become some sort of refuge for every leper, every barefoot or homeless man to spend the night—and that's not all. It was also perfectly clear that it was out of the question, absolutely out of the question to give an advance to an employee when you had no idea who or what he was, a person with no social status, when no one knows him, a man who's here today and tomorrow—gone to hell in a handbasket. And Mrs. Aaronson sank, finally, into one of the chairs, leaning back against the soft upholstery and closing her eyes wearily.

"No, sirs," she spoke in a broken, pained voice, shaking her head back and forth and sighing. "Say what you will—this is ingratitude, ingratitude of the most egregious sort; a person wants to put an end to his life—he has his choice of all those empty fields outside the city, of any number of abandoned houses and forests. So why and for what purpose, I ask you, does he come and disturb the peace and poison the lives of people who have done him no harm, *no harm,*" and here the lady buried her face in the elegant palms of her hands and her shoulders trembled and shook with suppressed sobs. The room fell into silence. From the street, a few isolated and muffled shouts arose from below, somebody calling the man of the house and urging him to hurry down, but his words were swallowed in the noise of the downpour and the banging of the shutters, which hadn't been properly latched that day. The house was chilly and dark and the odor of beds that hadn't been aired— and sadness—lingered. The maids stood beside the threshold with their hands tucked under their aprons and a great bewilderment in their eyes; and Shlomo Aaronson, who now emerged from his private office in his rustling autumn outfit, rubber boots on his feet, glanced at the guests drinking tea with cream at his table, looked over at his sobbing wife, raised his eyes to the gray heavens—and stood silent.

From downstairs, meanwhile, the bookkeeper's folded note

was brought up, a note scribbled in cramped and crooked letters, full of complaints and laments about how hard life was, about twenty straight years of empty solitude—no mother or father, no home, no light or warmth at all—about going from bad to worse, about being spit at in the face, straight in the face, and about all sorts of things like that, and all this—to some precious, dearly beloved sister.

And even though the people reading the note were quite solemn, far from any thought of obscenity or such, now, as they read this, they had a hard time stifling the smile that twitched and tugged at the corners of their lips.

For—sad to say—"sisters" of that sort were a dime a dozen among the help nowadays. Try going out when it was starting to get dark, just about then, just to see those creatures popping up on every sidewalk and square and wandering around, waiting for the minute when the businesses would close, when their guardian angels would show up to walk them home—these redeemers, whose salaries sometimes barely approached the princely sum of fifteen rubles a month, and who—Madame Aaronson will kindly excuse us—and whose toes were plainly visible through the holes in their shoes . . .

And in fact Mrs. Aaronson did kindly excuse them—as per their request; she rubbed her migraine-gripped temples with eau de toilette—and she excused them, and then she ordered the maids to bring rolls and bagels, hard- and soft-boiled eggs to the table, since, in the final analysis, one must eat a proper breakfast, and it was high time for doing so, too.

And after two hours, when the guests had gone off to their respective homes, and everything in the dining room had been washed and polished and put back in its place—Mr. Shlomo

Aaronson stood at the entrance of his warehouse, dressed from head to toe in raingear and with a large, open umbrella protecting him from above—talking with the local constable. Outside there was a lot of watery muck, and rain fell ceaselessly, and it was cold and gray, and the people walking by were hunched over, diminished, shivering. The naked trees trembled by the side of the street, and dogs wandered about abandoned, sodden—and Shlomo Aaronson stood there detailing to the constable the reasons why it was essential, it was crucial that the body of the deceased be removed from the warehouse.

And in fact after a brief explanation the policeman did understand that it was important to clear out the office and remove the dead man from there, a matter he accomplished without any great effort; the bookkeeper Levi Levine had been, as stated above, an extremely thin and short man, and therefore not especially heavy, and the constable, after he had lifted him from the floor and briefly taken in the strange expression on his face, tucked him under his arm (the workers and the other riffraff from the street, seeing the body in such a disposition, hands and feet dangling, head lolling—shrank back for some reason and shut their eyes), laid him in the wagon, and covered him with a mat. A few buckets of water and a mop for scrubbing the floor and washing the desks were brought into the store, and the shopkeepers, once the wagon and the body and mat that were in it had disappeared, dispersed each to his own shop; but Shlomo Aaronson ordered his workers to do this or that, put the account ledgers in order, and locked them up, went upstairs to his house, and stretched himself out on his sofa. During this time the wind outside had been growing stronger by the minute, raindrops mixed with hail were drumming on the tin roof above and against the glass panes of the windows and doors—which made it doubly delicious to lie on the soft sofa, to feel the pleasant warmth rising from the stove, the cleanliness and order of the room. In the next room the children were fooling around, cooing like a pair of love-birds, from the kitchen wafted the odor of stew cooking, the soothing hiss of fat sizzling in the frying pan, and the voice of the mistress of the house—and one would have to suppose that the impression of the entire drama, of the bookkeeper who went into the office, sat before the open ledgers, and committed suicide, had dissipated and been forgotten and erased from the minds of the members of the household on that very same day (since, in the final analysis, how difficult was it to find a clerk? They weren't exactly rare, these young people who came around these days knocking on every door looking for work), if it weren't for a minor incident that happened later that evening.

And that evening, the incident happened in this way:

At precisely seven-thirty, while the entire Aaronson family was sitting around the large table eating dinner, the sound of the doorbell was suddenly heard from the foyer, a chime that had been rung, from the sound of it, by a feeble and uncertain hand. And after some resistance and hesitation on the part of the maid, who both wanted and did not want to open the door for the person who had rung, a young girl entered the dining room, thin and short, and her face—was the face of the book-keeper Levi Levine. This was the sister of the suicide, without a doubt, and it now appeared that he had been unfairly suspected of sweet-talking and spilling his heart out in his note to some strange girl, as young men these days are wont to do. And a ponderous silence settled over the room.

For a moment the man of the house stirred in his seat, took the bookkeeper's letter from his pocket, and was about to rise— but then he remained in his seat, setting his fork on the edge of the plate before him.

"Maybe it would be a good idea to stand up and offer her that money, the advance her brother asked for," he eyed the miserable creature, who had dropped onto one of the chairs— and then he turned to gaze at his wife.

At that very moment the electricity came on above, in all the large and small ceiling lamps; the light in the room turned rich and bright, and the drawn face of the visitor dressed in rags now appeared in all its pallor, and it would have been a good idea if the governess had immediately taken the two children, Petya and Matya, out to their room and had calmed and entertained them (for example, she could have told them some nice fairy tale, with an instructive moral at the end) until the crisis had passed—until everyone could return to the table and continue the meal. But that was not done—either because of laziness or ignorance of the principles of pedagogy, be that as it may—and the girl who had been at first sitting on the chair with a lowered head, submissive and apparently in control of her emotions, suddenly rose from her place, and with trembling lips and palms oddly outspread she began running about here and there: "Oy, oy, her only brother, her poor brother," with such wails that the maids beside the door couldn't resist her and had to bury their faces in their aprons.

It was they who later reported (maids are great fibbers, of

course, but all the same) that that girl, after she had left the house, paused and stood by the locked warehouse, hitting her head against the iron bars, pulling her hair and crying her eyes out and complaining so bitterly that it just broke your heart, and all of this in the cold downpour and the pitch dark.

Somehow—at the home of the businessman Shlomo Aaronson the peace was disturbed on that evening too, and also throughout the entire following day. For the mistress of the house was in a bad state, an ugly mood, and she wouldn't leave her bedroom, and the children walked around with anxious faces, asking strange and annoying questions; and Shlomo Aaronson—walking back and forth within the room, walking and stumbling, walking and bumping up against the soft carpets underfoot—raised his eyes from time to time to the skies growing darker outside, stubbed out and lit one cigarette after another—and didn't say a word.

The End of Sender Ziv

In a foldout postcard from his little shtetl, Sender Ziv's younger sister, the married one, once asked him when his troubles and wanderings in the distant foreign city would finally come to an end.

The grave, she wrote to him, their father's grave, had been without a stone or marker for over two years now. The bundle of bed linen and few copper pots were piled in the pawnbroker's attic and there was not a soul who could redeem them, not a soul; and you know, just that week their wealthy cousin had returned from the city and whom had he bumped into there but Sender her brother, and he had seen him walking around the city the picture of gloom, dressed in rags, because he had no tutoring jobs to support him and no hope of getting his diploma, no prospects at all—and when, she would like to know, would all of this finally end? Wasn't it high time already?

And Sender Ziv, walking around the city after that, the

picture of gloom, dressed in rags, crumpling the foldout post-card he had received from his shtetl, thought that his younger sister, the married one, was absolutely right, and that his troubles and wanderings in the distant and foreign city should come to an end, since it was high time already.

This happened one fine morning at the end of winter, in the municipal park where the snow was melting on the ground and dripping from the trees above, and the birds chirped among the branches and everything was open, so wide open that the white stone house, Dr. Starkman's house across the park, could be seen there now in all its imposing height, with its odd-shaped balconies on the right and left and the French doors beside them—and Sender Ziv walked back and forth along the park boulevards and thought about the entrance examinations that were inexorably approaching, and about the daughter of his widowed landlady, who was at that very moment inside the large house, Dr. Starkman's house across the way, and he also thought about a few other things, and he hoped with all his heart that the winter would soon be over for good, that the French doors in the large stone houses would open wide and the doors of the gymnasium too, and spring would bloom over the earth and also in his heart, because that was how it was supposed to be, because it was high time already.

Later on, when the examinations had come and gone and with them, the spring, and the municipal park was bursting with heavy lush greenery, and the trees were so thick there was no way to see through them—Sender Ziv's pleasant dreams evaporated and his hopes melted like the chocolate bar he had once bought for the landlady's daughter, which melted in his pocket because he never gave it to her; as evening fell and the church bells slowly chimed and soft sorrow and darkness descended and on the sidewalks below strolled tall soldiers, enjoying a cigarette and chatting and laughing with the fair young landladies' daughters—Sender Ziv knew that there was no point in thinking about the end that his sister had written about, that Sender Ziv had no business talking or dreaming about any ending happy or otherwise, because for him, all endings had come and gone.

Rachel Feinberg, the elderly private tutor Rachel Feinberg, who had taken the exams along with Sender Ziv and had also failed by one mathematics problem, entered his room at one such twilight hour and the sight that appeared before her eyes shook her so deeply that she remained transfixed at the door and couldn't move from the spot.

Sender Ziv, short and gaunt, sat shrunken and alone at the large desk, his face buried in the textbooks before him, and his body shook with such odd shudders that it looked as if he were in the throes of some kind of seizure.

For a moment the tutor considered slipping away before her friend could notice her there, but then she changed her mind and approached him slowly, putting out her hand and gently touching his hair.

Mr. Ziv, she said to him, Mr. Ziv, perhaps it would be better if the gentleman were to go back to his old place, to the widow Malkin's house on the other side of the city?

There was no answer. He continued to sit, short and gaunt, at the large desk before him and he did not answer. And then Miss Feinberg took out her book, the thin math workbook she had brought with her from home, sank into one of the chairs before her—and lowered her head.

At such moments, the room was plunged into deep gloom.

By the fading daylight that penetrated the nearby window one could just make out the linked rows of math problems and the solitary numbers that were penciled in here and there on the grid of the workbook—faint, insecure numerals that leaned weakly on the question marks beside them, awaiting some kind of solution, some flash of insight . . .

They were thorny and difficult, indeed, the problems Rachel Feinberg had recently been encountering in her math workbook, but—how could she turn to him, her friend Sender, for help and explanations when his face was so dark and his body shuddered so oddly in the twilight?

On the contrary, as she sat later that night beside her open window, and in the alleyway below it was quiet and cool, and above, atop the nearby telegraph pole, an electric streetlight gazed at her, a single pale light—she struggled for a long time in her mind, devising solutions and strategies to rescue Sender Ziv from his thorny dilemma, to help him as much as she could and lighten his burden of sorrow.

True, the alleyway beside which Miss Feinberg sat was pleasantly cool and quiet, and the electric streetlight's pale blue glow was capable of arousing a whole range of thoughts and emotions—nevertheless the remembered image of the widow's daughter and her delicate face did not fade but rather continued to hover before her, together, mingling with his, with her friend and comrade Sender.

Sitting like that in the night before her open window, feeling endlessly and infinitely lonely, silent good tears would sometimes well in her eyes, tears of melancholy joy, as she envisioned this sweet couple, who in her imagination were bound with the bonds of true love, bound for all eternity, while behind them stood the soldier, a relative and admirer of the widow's daughter, sullen and seething, smoking his cigarette, the smoke rings curling and rising and dissipating in the breeze along with the hope in his heart.

Was it so impossible that the hopes of a young soldier, a tall heroic figure, whose mustache was huge and self-confidence immense—was it so impossible that even his hopes should sometimes go up in smoke, up in smoke like his cigarette?

She, Rachel Feinberg, one morning after finishing her lessons, the private lessons she gave in various houses, sat in the tram that went out to the other end of the city, got off at one of the street corners there, rented herself a small narrow room, and moved in that very day with her books and a few other meager possessions.

For a long time she kneeled before her open trunk, a large bachelor's trunk, and took out her writing implements and books, which she had packed with great haste and in no particular order and which she now had to arrange on the tables and bookshelves around.

She carried out this task slowly and heavily, for beside the books, textbooks she needed, over the years she had come to own various other objects, old and forgotten objects: postcards and photographs whose images had already faded with age; linens that her mother had sewn for her many, many years ago; a black hat with a thin veil, a mourning hat purchased after the death of her mother; and, finally, a brief note with a few comments on an essay that she had once received, at examination time, from him, her friend Sender.

Indeed, the memories aroused in her by all these objects that had come her way were difficult and sad. She carefully took them out of the trunk one after the other and laid them on the floor around her. And so she mutely kneeled for a while frozen above them, like a person gazing at the wreckage of their life.

But when nightfall approached she hurried to shake off the cobwebs of memories and gloom, prepared and poured herself a pot of tea on the little burner and went out to greet Sender Ziv, who had promised, who was supposed to stop by and see her new lodgings.

Although this room, the new one, was small and narrow, much smaller than the one she had had in the other neighborhood, and the stairs that led to the upper stories were also narrow and dilapidated, it made up for it with its large, well-appointed windows, and below, in the expanse that opened up before these windows, lay the park and all the streets and alleys around it, the rows of houses, large white stone houses beyond it and the gardens, flower gardens, beside these houses.

Is it really necessary to list the names of all these streets and alleys?

Through one of these windows the little garden, Dr. Starkman's flower garden, across from the big park, could be seen in exquisite detail, the garden with its narrow footpaths of freshly raked sand that wound their way among the flower beds and the governess, the Starkman children's governess, who was now strolling along those sandy paths.

There you go! It wasn't true, then, that the widow's daughter always made use of the free hour she had every evening to get together with her soldier cousin and stroll along the residential sidewalks with him.

Sender Ziv stood before the open window, before this amazing sight which spread out in front of him, and he closed and rubbed his eyes from time to time like a person who has just raised his face and gazed directly into the naked sun. He paced the length and width of the room a few times and then he stood, slowly passing his hand over his face and over his hair, a strange thought flickering through his mind with lightning speed, a thought so weird that it later shook him to the core.

He thought that if a war were to suddenly break out between Russia and some other country like the one, for example, a few years ago with Japan and so forth, if something like that happened, he thought—what would become of all the soldiers in this city?

Yes, that was what this whole thing had come down to. He, Sender Ziv, the tender-hearted, who wouldn't hurt a fly, the same human being who had been a strict vegetarian for years now, never touching the flesh of a living creature—he stood here, beside this window, and dreamed of bloodshed and men at war!

It was true—he tried to excuse himself—that it was only a momentary thought, a thought that flashed through his mind like the glitter of a sword and then disappeared, but even so— he had crossed a line—willfully and maliciously—so was there any point after that in standing here, beside the window, feeding his eyes on the beauty that lay before him?

Pale with excitement he took his walking stick and hat in hand, ran down the stairs by the light of matches that Rachel Feinberg lit one after another behind him, and for the first time in many long weeks, he crossed the spacious square that opened into the park and entered its arbors and flower beds.

One of Sender Ziv's acquaintances, an external student who penned stories that he submitted to a Hebrew literary journal, mocked Sender Ziv and shrugged his shoulders when the latter unburdened his secret love once to him.

Believe me, my friend, the young storyteller told him, that if we were to put down in writing a description of a bachelor over thirty, a man with no social position and no solid ground beneath his feet, dried up and dirt poor, losing more of his hair every day, a broken shell of a man, and he, this bachelor, his only ambition is just for the shadow of a fair young girl, and he daydreams about her and paces underneath her window at night like a schoolboy—if we were to write like that, they would say that we were falsifying reality, that this was fanciful and beneath criticism, since no bachelor who was over thirty, a dried-up and dirt-poor man who was losing more of his hair every day, and who was a broken shell of a man, this man would daydream only of a quiet corner room in an attic, the landlady's spinster daughter, and a grocery—just a small store with a sign that wasn't too big and a home-cooked hot meal, which the mother-in-law would cook and serve him with her own two hands.

Or maybe he, Sender Ziv, was still hoping to keep studying, to finally get a diploma from a good gymnasium and with it some decent position in life?

No, to study, to keep studying to pass examinations and acquire diplomas was not something he was capable of right now, not right now. He, Sender Ziv, had never sent a story to a newspaper or journal, and he had never thought about whether he was being true to life or falsifying reality, but the fact that his heart swelled inside him and choked him with pain and longing no less than the heart of some schoolboy—of that there could be not the slightest doubt.

Yes, the metropolis had fallen into a great ennui in the last few days and a suffocating atmosphere hung over everything. Each day carriages full of furniture and housewares rolled by along the banks of the river toward the neighboring forest, to the spacious summer homes within it. One by one the large stone houses emptied out and were shut and bolted, the houses with their little gardens and gazebos—and Sender Ziv paced the sidewalks stumbling with exhaustion, walking and raising his eyes to the windows of the closed houses above, and the thoughts withered and crumbled in his head like the flowers in the abandoned gardens beside the houses around him.

At dusk, with the chiming of the large bells in the monastery and church towers, the riverbank surged with young and old people who pushed and hurried into the small boats, which lay waiting to sail off to the various summer resorts. Far, far away, on the slopes of the hills across the river, darkened the forest, the large pine forest, along whose wide arbors young boys and girls were now hiking morning and evening, and in the meadow beside those arbors children of all ages formed groups, their fresh white shirts flashing in the sunlight while they played croquet alongside gangly gymnasium students and fair young governesses.

Rachel Feinberg stood before her window, the window of her new room, which faced the park and the streets around it, and strands of thin hair escaped her scanty bun, falling listlessly down her neck.

Here, within the small room, stood her large trunk, the bachelor's trunk, in complete disarray. The old photographs lay strewn about, their images blurred and abandoned. Her rumpled and dusty linen was thrown over a chair, and against the white linen, the old felt mourning hat stood out in dark contrast, stirring distant memories and hard melancholy.

Sender Ziv, pacing back and forth in this small room, would stop occasionally before the pile of linen—beside the hat, secretly stroking its silky smooth ribbons and veil, and during those moments his thin face would grimace and darken, to a much deeper shade even than the mourning band he was fingering.

What was it with Sender Ziv at those moments, and why did his face darken so? Were black thoughts flickering in his heart, thoughts of death and oblivion? Or perhaps the sight of that hat aroused in him memories of other days, the days when the widow's daughter was in mourning, when she would wear a felt hat and veil as black as this one—and he was still safely ensconced in her house, basking in the glory of her presence every day? Who knows?

She, Rachel Feinberg, after standing once for many hours over her trunk folding and rearranging everything in it, went down to the riverbank and bought herself a ticket for the evening boat; and at seven that evening, as the monastery bells around were chiming and the pier surged with the crowds of young and old people, she too pushed her way down to the harbor below, the hatbox she had filled with books in hand and a glimmer of grace in her eyes, and she climbed on board the boat that was sailing off to the large pine forest.

As the boat started to move, she took a small white handkerchief out of her pocket to wave it in the air a few times and smiled cheerfully.

She had not yet found a place to sit, she was still holding onto the hatbox, which swayed along with the movements of the boat, but—no matter: she gazed at him, at Sender Ziv, with her large, kind eyes, waving her handkerchief at him—and she smiled:

"Won't the gentleman come soon to visit me in the forest?" she called to him as the boat swung around to face upriver, and Sender Ziv looked at her—at the small handkerchief in her hand and at the sloping hills beyond that handkerchief, and suddenly he felt acutely that if he didn't hurry to get away from this harbor and from these people around him, they would all witness the same thing that had once overcome him in his room, the time Miss Feinberg had come to see him and he had forgotten to close his door properly.

"Won't the gentleman come soon to visit me in the forest?" his long-suffering friend, his hard-luck, good-hearted comrade-in-exams.

Sitting a little while later on a solitary forsaken bench at the end of the pier, with the river crouched wide and lazy and brimming at the banks, and everything around was thick with sadness, shadow, and the chiming of bells—there arose before him in turns her face, dark, near, his friend in sorrow, in complicated math problems, and the face of the other one, bright, radiating light, but distant, herself as complicated as a math problem for which there was no solution at hand, and no place even to begin, none at all.

Memories of the not-so-distant past swam up before him now like isolated torches within a dark abyss: Friday nights in that house, the widow's house, the warm stove and the warmth of family life. She, the daughter, the widow's daughter who had come to visit her mother's house, two fair braids fluttering down her back, and the pure light streaming from her eyes, a light that could warm a soul as frozen as his, Sender Ziv's, encouraging it and stirring confidence and faith within it. For if that light had not suddenly dimmed for him and flickered out—who knows if he might not already have gotten back on his feet and found a position in life, a position that would have made him the envy of every external student and scribbler of stories.

Oh, the thoughts that raced through the heart of Sender Ziv on this summer evening, sitting on the solitary bench at the end of the pier, as the river crouched before him lazy and wide and brimming at the banks.

The shadows around him, though, were darkening with every passing moment. The vision of the hills across the river slowly faded, swallowed by the mist. The chiming of the bells in the church tower also faded away, but in their place now came from one of the nearby houses the tinkling of a sad piano, fragments of a song, a song that had the power to pull the heartstrings and make the tears flow in any young damsel's eyes. And Sender Ziv sat and thought that if only he had the talent to express his emotions in verse, like the poet who had composed this song, then—who knows?—maybe he could write something that would bring tears to the eyes of girls whose hearts were set as stone against him.

But he did not have the gift of expressing himself in words, no. He couldn't write, develop his thoughts on paper, not even as well, for example, as that kind spinster, the external student Rachel Feinberg, who not long after began to write and send him short beautiful letters from the summer resort every day and who, with great economy and simplicity, conveyed to him news of various acquaintances, male and female, but especially of Chana Malkin, the widow's daughter and governess Chana Malkin, who arose so early in the hot summer morn, going out to the forest, into the depths of the forest at dawn's early light, while the mist still hung heavy and opaque all around and the shutters of every house were still securely bolted.

And here too, she wrote to him, there are small flower gardens beside the larger houses and gazebos and paths, narrow footpaths strewn with sand where one could go for a pleasant stroll at sunset.

In the leafy arbors deep within the forest it was almost always dark and quiet, a cool and sweet darkness, but at the same time the large meadow near these arbors, by Dr. Starkman's house, was full of radiant sunlight and children of all ages and the doctor's children, led by their governess—was there any need to ask him yet again if he would pay a visit here soon? Certainly he would come, her "soul brother"—she finished her letter with a quote from Nadson's poetry.

Yes, indeed he would: "The weary and tormented."

"The weary and tormented soul brother!"

Sender Ziv stood by the small mirror hanging on the wall before him, looking into it as he hastily shaved his beard, and his hands trembled and slipped repeatedly on his smooth face, as if he were preparing for an oral exam before a committee of teachers. His new satin shirt, the shirt he had bought yesterday expressly for this trip, was uncomfortable, strange in its rustle and brightness, too bright, perhaps, for his thirty years, for his sorrow—for that quotation, so perfectly apt, from the poetry of Nadson.

But the morning breeze later, as he boarded the boat, bolstered his spirits and steadied his hands again. The boat sailed through the smell of the surrounding fields and the abundant light and wide expanses, the kind of expanses he had experienced only many, many years before, on the outskirts of that faraway shtetl when he went with his friends to gather greenery for the Shavuot festival—and rather than stanzas of Russian poetry, there flashed now in his memory forgotten passages from the texts of his distant childhood, entire verses of the Psalms and the Song of Songs. How insipid and humdrum now seemed the metropolis he was leaving behind on the riverbank, and how flimsy and unthreatening those military barracks in the suburbs beyond it.

Rachel Feinberg, who had come out to meet him on the bank with her white parasol, and who then brought him, Sender Ziv, under said parasol, paused for a moment when the two of them reached the top of the slope, stretched out her hand and showed him the city, squatting there so low now, blackened by soot and dust, while here, on this side, she gestured, everything is drenched in the sweetness of summer and the bounty of the Lord above.

And indeed the place was beautiful, with its thick profusion of pines and the blaze of its colorful flowers, its towering peaks and the rush of its streams, the hidden streams that coursed through these mountains.

And yes, beside the great houses were small flower gardens, and there were gazebos in these gardens and paths, narrow footpaths strewn with the finest golden sand.

In the arbors deep within the forest reigned silence and shadow, a cool sweet dimness, while the large meadow near these arbors, by Dr. Starkman's house, was full of brilliant sunshine and children of all ages, especially the doctor's children with their governess at the head, she with her two fair braids tumbling down her back and a delicate azure silk ribbon entwined in those braids.

"Had he come here too, to this place of ours?" she asked Sender Ziv, shaking her head so that her two braids shimmered a little behind her, and it occurred to him, Sender Ziv, that all the splendor flowing around him here came not from above, from the sun in the sky, but rather from her, from this widow's daughter standing before him, from the gold of the braids that hung down her back, from between the folds of delicate azure ribbon entwined in those braids.

Was there any point in going on now?

Rachel Feinberg, who was waiting for him in one of the nearby lanes, handed him the flowers she had been gathering here among the trees and from her own flower bed, the one small flower bed that lay outside the window of her room—and she walked silently along beside him, withdrawn under her open parasol, looking every once in a while at the bouquet that was growing and growing, spilling through and twining around the fingers of her friend.

A shame about those flowers she had picked from her flower

bed, the one flower bed that lay outside the window of her room: on her bed, later that night, she buried her face in her small pillow for a long time, her hard, spinster pillow, and tears streamed unceasingly, tirelessly, from her eyes, while at the same time, in another room, the vacant room nearby, Sender Ziv sat by the light of the lamp, rearranging yet again the large bouquet before him.

He took one of her most recent letters and shaded the burning lamp with it to keep the light from penetrating the nearby room and disturbing his friend's sleep, and so he sat, motionless and shrouded in shadow, over his books and the colorful bouquet before him, and he would nod off, falling into a web of dreams.

Unhurriedly, the images streamed by him one at a time. Strange and distant fields appeared; wide-open skies, the skies over his shtetl; and his father's grave, an abandoned grave, in truth, with no marker or stone, but nevertheless swathed in light and serenity, and his father gazing at him from within his grave and he, too—his face was glowing and serene:

"Good luck, my son, Godspeed," he nodded and looked at him with enormous compassion, and the strange distant fields stretched out, streaming onward and disappearing, the fields and the skies over his shtetl and the grave, his father's grave. There was nothing but a great radiance and peace, and from within this splendor and expanse swam up a close and familiar image, the image of his former landlady's daughter, the widow Malkin's daughter: tall and light of step—slowly and rhythmically she walked toward him, walking and nodding, and her two fair braids hanging and quivering on her back like the small golden earrings that hung in her ears.

"Chana, Chana," he called out her name, "do you know what brought me here, to this pine forest?"

She nodded:

Yes, she knew.

"And the agonies of my soul for lo this whole year now and more, you also knew?"

"That too."

"Would you like me to bring you the bouquet of flowers I picked for you with my own hands?"

"Later, this morning, along the ridge path," she replied, turning her head and disappearing, and with her disappeared also the splendor and expanse around them—and the room was filled with the dark shadows of early morning.

Sender Ziv arose, ran his hand over his face and through his unkempt hair, and went out.

The fog that lay around was still dark, opaque, and the shutters on every house were securely bolted:

What did those words mean, "Good luck, Godspeed?" What was the road on which he, Sender Ziv, was preparing to embark, and why had his father looked at him with such enormous compassion?

Along the lanes morning was already stirring, peasant men and women passing along the trails bringing produce from the nearby farms. It was almost five o'clock. From the closest trail came the rustle of a dress, a familiar, gentle, sweet rustle—and he lengthened his stride and turned into the ridge path.

Suddenly it sounded like a muffled song and the sound of footsteps was coming from that same trail. They were heavy footsteps, without a doubt the footsteps of a man, and the song—a military tune, a barracks chant, and for a moment he stood dumbfounded and listened.

"Are there any army camps around here?" he asked a peasant coming his way.

And then it happened, the thing which momentarily startled all the peasants who made their living selling milk and vegetables around here and which the locals gossiped about for days and weeks to come: Sender Ziv, taking a look at the soldier who was now visible walking toward him through the underbrush, suddenly started and lurched backward. For an instant it seemed that he was about to escape into a nearby trail, which was across from him now, but then he changed his mind and flinched violently and, losing his balance, slowly pitched backward from the ridge path and tumbled to the boulders below, where he lay, his body a broken shell.

To Sender Ziv it seemed in the moment he flinched that someone had shoved him and sent him along with a vulgar curse—in army slang. But the sensation of that shove and the curse that followed flitted through his mind for only a moment, no longer. Then came other impressions, then the river below appeared, with the two sloping banks on his right and on his left and the profusion of light and expansive ease on the face of these slopes, an ease he had felt only many long, long years ago, at the outskirts of that faraway shtetl, when he would go out with his friends to gather greenery for the Shavuot festival. Finally they also appeared, those very same good friends: flooded with light and filled with compassion—one after the other they broke out of the reeds below, walking toward him from the depths, they came, spreading their small arms out to receive him—and around him was rest, sweet rest, comforting rest—like the rest that comes only after the solution has been found to a difficult and complicated problem.

Rachel Feinberg, as she hiked after that in the days that followed among the shrubbery and boulders below, at the foot of the mountain, discovered there, along with an old straw hat and shreds of a satin shirt, a few stray flowers that were strewn here and there among the weeds and looked as worthless and dried out as the bloodstains around them. They were the flowers of the bouquet, the same bouquet that he, her friend Sender, had gathered so tenderly and obsessively only a few hours before he met his end.

Not very long after that the rest of the flowers somehow wilted too, the flowers in the one flower bed outside the window of her room—either because of neglect or because autumn was approaching—and she, Rachel Feinberg, gathered her few belongings and her schoolbooks, left and went back to the big city, the nearby city, and took up residence again in her old apartment, in the old building on the alley.

As she sat every night beside her open window, lonely, endlessly and infinitely lonely, the trace of Sender Ziv's face would often rise before her, with his strikingly radiant countenance as he stood by the large meadow near the forest arbors.

Well, she thought, sometimes after the most horrific death agonies, a person finds relief in the moment before he dies. And he sees himself happy and content and thinks that his life is only beginning at that moment—Sender Ziv had a moment like that, as he stood beside the open meadow by the forest arbors, a moment that came to him only after he had suffered death pangs for thirty years or more.

The alleyway beside which Miss Feinberg was sitting was pleasantly cool and quiet, and there was an electric streetlight hanging above her window, a light that cast a pale blue glow capable of arousing a whole range of thoughts and emotions— but even so she no longer remembered the widow's daughter pure and clear in her heart as she once had, and when her face appeared now before her meditating eyes it always appeared together, side by side, with the broad-chested soldier whose heart was so hard, while at the same time, behind them, lay only a dark lonely grave, a grave over which the earth was still freshly turned—there had been no time for it to dry.

Rachel Feinberg visited Sender Ziv's grave very frequently. It was set a little way off from the rest of the graves in the cemetery, unmarked and without a stone, like his father's in the distant shtetl.

In the autumn the crows would come and stand on the moist earth, pecking with their beaks and shrieking—and then Rachel Feinberg would take her small handkerchief, bury her face in it for a long time, and tears would stream from her eyes, while the wind struggled and moaned in the nearby trees, shaking withered leaves off the branches and strewing them on the ground below.

Once, when she was returning from the cemetery on an autumn day like that, something fairly minor happened to her that nonetheless succeeded in unduly agitating her: the governess, the widow's daughter, Miss Chana Malkin, who was passing on the sidewalk, seemed to rest her eyes on her for a moment as if she were on the verge of saying something. It was at sunset. In the church towers the large bells were slowly chiming and a soft melancholy and shadow were all around, and she, Rachel

Feinberg, was walking and thinking with satisfaction about how she was managing to cut expenses, scraping together a little money so that soon she would be able to order a headstone for the grave, even if only a simple headstone with the cheapest inscription, in small letters—and suddenly it seemed to her that the widow's daughter, who was approaching, was looking at her and wanting to say something, and a faint tremor passed through her, and she gathered up her nerve and was about to walk over to her; but the next moment she became convinced that it wasn't she who had drawn the girl's attention but her hat—the black felt hat sitting on her head, the one that so resembled the widow's daughter's mourning hat which had always drawn the attention of the deceased, Sender Ziv—and then she hurried on, stepping quickly off the curb and turning to cross to the other side of the street.

Liska

Skinny and with a short, raggedy tail—she would make her way like a meek lamb among the bowls of meat and schmaltz in the gulch kitchens, absorbing the delicious aromas and swallowing back her saliva as if she didn't have two rows of sharp teeth in her mouth and the impulses of a dog in her heart.

What did she need an owner's whistle for? Why did she need to beg? When the moment came that we, the youngest schoolchildren, were unleashed from school—along she would come and stretch out at our feet, front and back paws extended, and she would bat her eyes and give her body over to the dozens of small hands, as if to say: "Take me, I'm yours, all yours."

And pieces of sausage, rolls soaked in milk, bagels and cakes would rain down on her from every bag and every pack.

"Just don't throw it all at once, not at the same time! Liska doesn't mix milk and meat."

It wouldn't be long before the dog was lying at the door to the synagogue hall, full and content. From there, from inside the study hall, clear, sweet voices reached her, the voices of the gulch children praying fervently, and she would cock both ears, close her eyes, and listen.

"So, Liska, should we go for a walk now?"

No. Liska had no interest in hiking. As soon as we, her friends, disappeared toward the riverbank, off she would go to some secluded corner, where she would stretch herself out luxuriously on the ground and commune with her soul.

What were the thoughts that percolated in her doggy brain at such moments? Was she reminiscing about the distant past, the days of her childhood and adolescence, which passed among the pots of curds and sour cream in the dairyman's house? Or was she remembering him, the estate owner's dog, whom she had loved so dearly in their youth, and her three tiny, swarthy pups, who had been stolen from her and whom she hadn't even been allowed to suckle . . .

Presumably thoughts like these, or similar ones, were passing through the dog's mind at the twilight hour. That must be why her head was lowered to the ground with such weary sorrow. But to let loose a bark against her luck, or to grumble and whine—that was not her way.

In general Liska rarely raised her voice in the gulch. For what? And biting was something she had no notion of at all: she was a modest dog, quiet and mild-tempered, a nice Jewish dog.

Only in the darkness of night, when the skies over town were thick and gloomy and everything around was pitch black, and something mysterious would spring out of the ominous stillness—Liska would sometimes be standing in the middle of the street, craning her neck upward toward the heavens, and from her mouth would emerge a muffled howl, muffled yet mournful, forlorn, heartrending. And at that moment one of the gulch folk would suddenly know that the Angel of Death hovered nearby, brandishing his sword over the head of a neighbor or friend, and trembling, that person would climb out of bed and strike his fist against the wall three times:

"Let this be on your head, Liska, on your head."

And Liska would listen, hang her head, and quietly, sadly slink off to the side of the street.

That there were, on the gentile street up the hill, vicious dogs with dagger-teeth and spear-claws—that was something we knew and Liska knew, too.

A loaded wagon might be coming down the road that descended from the hill to the gulch. The driver is bone-weary, his face drenched in perspiration and his knees buckling, the wheels of the wagon squeaking and squealing as they bump over the rocks and broken branches in the road, and the horse—with the last of his strength he would be trudging heavily along—and suddenly dozens upon dozens of dogs spring out from every direction, all of them swift and agile, all of them arrogant, brazen, and evil, and the whole pack of them fall upon the driver and his horse:

"Arf-arf, arf-arf, arf-arf!"

Liska, standing at a distance, raises her head a little, straining her eyes to see, and then suddenly—she tucks her short tail between her legs, her whole body shrinks down and she starts racing down the main street, through the alley where the poorest people live, taking shortcuts over fences and roofs, moving from one yard into another, panting and heaving, her haunches rising and falling, rising and falling:

What was happening to her? Who was she so afraid of?

In the gulch they used to tell the story:

Liska had been hurt by those vicious dogs a long time ago, when she was still living at the dairyman's outside town. Loyal and devoted to her owner, she stood guard night after night, always keeping an eye peeled especially for the uphill folk, who were known to be thieves.

Once, on a particularly dark night, Liska sensed silent footfalls inside the yard. She immediately opened her mouth to bark, but then something strange happened: Two strong hands grabbed her from behind, pushed her head into a narrow sack and began dragging her over sticks and stones, over thistles and thorns, far, far away from the dairyman and his yard.

Where were they taking her? What was going on? What was going to happen to her owner's yard? Pots and basins were hung out to dry over every fence post. And on a dark and gloomy night like this . . .

Not long after that Liska recognized, with sorrow, that she had been taken captive among the gentiles: a small house with a low ceiling, a trough full of vegetable scraps, snorting piglets, and the smell of cabbage stewing in lard . . . She felt trapped: she was surrounded by strangers, utter strangers . . . These rascals were pursing their lips at her and whistling, as if she were one of their own. One of them threw her a heel of coarse bread smeared with cooked blood. It just sickened her. She wasn't used to such stuff, a Jewish dog . . . So she slunk off to a corner, curled herself into a ball, and shut her eyes . . . Suddenly she heard an eerie, grating bark:

"Grkh-grkh!" The sound was like a swarm of stinging bees, buzzing around her: "Grrrkh-rkh-rkh!"

It was the uphill dogs, that evil-begotten pack, surrounding the house, thudding against the door, and snarling at the owner of the house to say:

"Let out that bitch who has entered your house, so that we may know her!"

Liska shuddered and opened her eyes. The old man, the man of the house, looked at her mockingly now and even the children laughed; the door was standing open ... Not a moment passed before two hands grabbed her by the ears and began dragging her out.

Many pairs of shining, lustful eyes peered out at her from within the darkness, falling on her from every side ...

The next day, as she lay along the slope of the hill aching and torn, her black fur matted and bloodstained and her heart filled with bile—she suddenly felt warm, soft hands upon her, caressing her with great compassion:

"Liska, Liska!" Someone was calling her by name, and the caresses came thicker and faster. "Liska, poor Liska, what happened to you?" and these words were spoken in her owner's language, in Yiddish ...

It was one of the gulch folk who happened to be up there and then brought her down here, to the Jewish street ...

And there was another story they told about her in the gulch:

The gentiles from up the hill grabbed Liska on Kol Nidre night, when no Jew was home, brought her uphill, and tried to make her eat pork. When she clenched her teeth and shut her mouth and even held her breath against the smell—they warned her:

"If you won't eat it, you can just sit right here and fast for three days and three nights."

And when, after these threats, they tried to stuff another piece of pork into her mouth—and she still wouldn't take it, they jammed her tail into the crook of a tree and set the dogs of the hill on her . . .

When she finally escaped from her abusers, wounded and bleeding, her stomach empty and her eyes searching to see from whence her salvation would come—before her eyes, at long last, appeared the gulch:

Small and crowded homes, a large bathhouse, piles of garbage in every yard and the scent of noodle kugel . . .

It was Sabbath. Little schoolchildren, freed from the yoke of Torah-study, came toward her in their little clusters, greeting her with cooked beans and peas, with dances and joyous laughter.

Then the dog turned her head toward the hill, let out a benedictory bark for her rescue—and felt herself even more strongly bound to the gulch than before.

It happened at the end of winter. The gulch river, frozen and contracted into itself, stretched out before us in all the radiance of its glistening ice, and we, armed with wooden boards in place of skates, ran and skidded back and forth with rosy faces and sparkling eyes. We had the day off from school, and the ice beneath our feet was still very solid, while a bright springlike sun gazed down from above, its rays caressing our faces and necks . . .

Our dog was with us too. Today she wouldn't have to wait for us at the schoolhouse door, and since there was still a little time before evening prayers—then let her be here with us, feasting her eyes on us while we, in turn, enjoyed ourselves with her.

This one holding her by the ears and that one by the tail, dragging her along on the crunchy snow, leaping and prancing before her, dancing around her in circles, scratching and tickling her, scratching and hugging her—singing all the while:

> Beautiful dog, you righteous beast!
> Tomorrow we'll cook you a kosher feast.
> Tra-la-la, tra-la-la . . .

And that was when something happened: The dog, quivering all over and covered with sweat, suddenly slipped from our grasp, and her neck shrank and shortened and her eyes began blinking rapidly, as if she were sensing danger.

"Liska, don't worry, we'll stick out our necks for you."

"Hee-hee. Ha, ha . . ."

She stared at us and we stared at her and the whole group of us turned our gaze toward the hill—and suddenly we were all shaking and clutching one another: from the hill, from the gentile street, a large black dog was leaping down toward us, his fur just as curly as could be—everything about him spelled insolence, and he bounded down toward us with the gangly joints of his immensity—his jaws agape. He ran with the fleetness of a deer and his bark was sheer terror.

Liska wobbled. For a moment she opened her mouth and started to let out a bark, but she quickly changed her mind and hung her head. Her paws shook and sagged and she dropped to the ground, stretching out completely as if she were saying: "What does all this have to do with me?"

But that fierce dog just came closer to her, barking: "Kho-kho-kho . . ."

And now Liska could no longer restrain herself. She suddenly raised her short tail, straightened her body, and—for the first time in her life—barked in protest:

"Arf-arf-arf," three times in succession but then, apparently, the sound of her own voice frightened her and she doubled into a half-crouch and began to scramble and run with all the strength in her thin legs toward the gulch. And she never once turned her head toward the river or toward the slope of the hill . . .

Still, from this point on the gentile dog began to visit the gulch. If Liska ever visited the hill—we didn't know. We, the children of the Jewish street, would threaten her and plead with her not to go to the gentile street, and she would raise her head and put on a modest face, as if she were saying: "If you want me to, I'll go into the hallway of the synagogue and lie there all day without moving a muscle" . . . But even so, every once in a while she would disappear for hours on end . . .

It was the season of the thaw. In every corner and at every step flowed glistening puddles, paper boats sailed down one gutter and up another, toy canoes were swept along in the stream . . . through the air rang the clatter of rolling pins and wafted the smell of warm matzoh, and the laughter of boys and the voices of young girls rang from one end of the gulch to another: spring, spring, spring. And the world of the Holy One, blessed be He, was so fine at that hour, and the outside chores so pleasant that no child noticed that the sun was already standing in the west, the horizon was reddening and fathers were appearing at the windows, tapping their fingertips on the panes to signal that the time had come for evening prayers.

And when the children emerged from the synagogue, they noticed that Liska was missing.

How could that be? After all, the bones near the butcher's had been piled up, drying out since that morning. Leftovers had been lying around on the garbage heap all day—and Liska was nowhere in sight.

From the west blew a warm mild breeze and far, far away a cracking sound could be heard; the Zhuzhik River, the river that flowed by the gulch, had split itself into many pieces and was threatening to flood the Jewish street. And it was a moonless night, a dark night. The heart shrank with worry: on such a night! Maybe some farmer had passed through here and dragged her after his horse and carriage to the other side of the river. Maybe the hooligans from up the hill had come down and taken her off—who knows! Should they go up to their street, to the gentile street? . . .

But—hush! There, in the snowdrifts on the slope of the hill, two black bodies were moving around. There, they stopped for a moment, raised their heads, and barked softly; the next moment they were moving again, climbing further and further up: Liska—in the company of that gentile dog . . .

A long row of uphill dogs was descending in a chain to meet them, accompanied by the wolf whistles of the hooligans—Oh, the shame of it, the disgrace of it.

And from then on Liska was utterly changed. She no longer waited for us at the gate to the synagogue yard or at the school-house. And she was no longer as sweet-tempered as she had once been. She learned to bark like the gentile dogs—and sometimes she would get up from her spot, sneak quietly into some kitchen, wait for the moment when the housewife would leave—and then—cursed were the eyes that witnessed such a thing—she would snatch the choicest cut of meat.

"Liska, Liska!"

She would drop to the ground, devour it, and wipe her mouth and her two eyes would flash with a strange glint.

"Oy vey."

"What would become of her?"

With aching hearts and sorrowful voices the children would ask each other that question.

And sometimes one of the mothers would notice her child's gloomy face, and trying to do something to cheer him up, she would say:

"Take this piece of bread for that dog of yours, go feed her!"

"Feed her yourself, if you want to," would come the angry response.

And when the night would later descend and dreams would seethe in the mind, each of us would see the gulch turned into a den of wild animals: a pack of stocky, curly-haired dogs, with powerful teeth and evil desires, and they were doing all sorts of vicious things here, unimaginably vicious things—just like the dogs on their street, the Christian street . . .

And shuddering, covered in sweat, each of us would awaken from sleep and the same black thought would chill our blood:

"Liska is no longer one of us."

That day a cracked and ragged sun went down in the west, and just as it set heavy, dark clouds appeared from some mysterious distant region and floated up on the horizon, and darkness descended.

Not one of the boys went down to the riverbank to smell the reeds and flowers.

"So, have you been to evening services yet?"

"Have you?"

And like mute shadows the boys stood inside the synagogue, separate and isolated, each boy in his own world. And silently and mournfully we girls stood behind the synagogue, listening to the sad chant of the congregants, to the "Orphan's Kaddish," while all eyes were fixed on the darkness in the distance.

"And you shall expunge the evil from amongst yourselves"— who had taught us that today? The rabbi at school? An older friend? Or maybe no one had said it at all . . .

And as if from some black abyss, pictures and stories from long ago rose and stood before our mind's eye, heroes from the holy books: Akhan with the bar of gold and Shinar mantle he had taken as spoils . . . His head was lowered and his eyes were cast to the ground, and a flood of stones rained down on his head, on his face, all over his sinning body: "What calamity you have brought down upon us! The Lord will bring calamity upon you this day." . . . And we remembered also the man and the Midianite woman pierced through with the spear of Pinchas, son of Elazar . . .

Thus shall they perish, thus shall they perish . . .

Liska lies before us on the ground, sinful and wallowing in her filthy deeds, and not one of us strokes her fur, not one of us graces her with a tender word.

The wicked thing! One after another she trampled those

little chicks walking around the gulch, shamelessly and disgracefully ... And there was the time with the poor sick man who had broiled himself a calf's liver for supper—and the greedy beast came along and robbed it from under his very nose ... And then there was the story about the little baby who was sitting and playing in the sand, holding a bagel smeared with butter—and she sprang out from nowhere and bit the baby's hand and devoured the bloodstained bagel ...

"Hss-s-s-s. Are we all here?"

Each of us steps forward quietly, tremulously, the heart inside each breast pounds powerfully, powerfully ...

The rope has already been slipped over one of the posts in the marketplace. It's long and thick and the end, tied in a noose, flutters like a black wing back and forth in the wind ...

"Where is she?!"

We all know that Liska is somewhere among us, but no one dares to put out a hand and grab her neck ... Her head hangs to the ground with such lackluster sorrow ...

"Hey, hey, hey, hey, hey, hey ..."

Was there some foreboding in her heart now?

Maybe the right thing to do was to let her go ... Let her grovel around behind some fence, excommunicated and barren. Or—let her go up that hill and blend right into that crowd of their dogs ...

"Stand on your hind legs, bitch!"

And she accepts the verdict.

"Put your head in the noose."

She doesn't resist.

Something rattles in the air, trembles once, and falls silent.

Black clouds creep across the sky. They're so heavy on your brain, they choke your throat.

"L-i-s-k-a! . . ."

And she, who had whimpered and howled at the death of each and every Jew in the gulch, herself died peacefully and in utter silence. Not a sigh escaped her throat.

GLOSSARY

BUBBE: Grandmother; or an affectionate term for an old woman

CHALLAH: braided loaf, made of fine flour, eaten on the Sabbath

CHEDER: one-room schoolhouse for small boys

CHUPPAH: wedding canopy, or the marriage ritual conducted beneath it

HALAKHA: the codified body of Jewish law

HAVDALAH: benediction over wine, a candle, and a spice box marking the conclusion of the Sabbath and the beginning of the week

KADDISH: memorial prayer praising God recited for deceased parents by a male descendant; in Yiddish colloquial usage, a son (who will recite the prayer after his parents' death)

KIDDUSH: benediction over the Sabbath wine, customarily recited by the male head of the household

KOL NIDRE: solemn prayer recited on the eve of Yom Kippur

KUGEL: baked Sabbath pudding or casserole, typically made of noodles or potatoes

MAZEL TOV: congratulations

MITZVAH: commandment, or good deed

MIZRACH: literally, east. Colloquially, a plaque, often of stained glass, to be hung on the eastern wall of a home or synagogue to indicate the direction of prayer—toward Jerusalem

OMER: the forty-nine days, ritually counted in the synagogue, between Passover and Shavuot (Pentecost)

REBBETZIN: a rabbi's wife

SCHMALTZ: chicken fat, used for a variety of dishes

SHAVUOT: the feast of Pentecost

SHEKHINA: the feminine Godhead

SHIVA: (Hebrew, "seven") the week of mourning after a death of a close relative

SHOFAR: a ram's horn, blown at synagogue services during the High Holy Days as a call to repentance

SHTETL: (Yiddish, "small town") Eastern European small town with a significant Jewish population; or the distinctive world, customs, and life of such small towns in Eastern Europe

TKHINE: Jewish women's supplication, in Yiddish rather than Hebrew, or a collection of such vernacular prayers

TORAH: the Five Books of Moses; the traditional Jewish library and the religious traditions embodied within them

YESHIVA: Talmudic academy

ZEYDE: Grandfather

Text: 11/15 Granjon
Display: Granjon
Composition: Binghamton Valley Composition
Printing and binding: Maple-Vail Book Manufacturing Group